"Unrequited love, at its best." - Femonomic

Diary of a Whimsical Lover

Gaurav Sharma

Diary of a Whimsical Lover

Gaurav Sharma

Title: Diary of a Whimsical Lover
Author: Gaurav Sharma
Published by: Think Tank Books in 2022
Address: RZ-26/27B, Ashok Park, West Sagarpur, New Delhi - 110046
Website: thinktankbooks.com
Email: editorial@thinktankbooks.com

Gaurav Sharma asserts the moral right to be identified as the author of this book.

ISBN: 978-93-91607-00-5
Price: INR 250/-
Retail price listed is only for the Indian subcontinent.
Selling price may vary elsewhere.

5 4 3 2 1

This book is based on true events.
Except for the parts that are totally made up.

Dedicated to SONY.
For keeping PlayStation 5 in global shortage.
Keep it that way & I'll start writing my next book.

Something that never happened before, happened!

Before I knew, the unprecedented had befallen.
The coagulated swamp that once swept me
Across my feet, disguising as cosmos
Was now engulfing me into its abyss.

The restraint had been gradually slithering.
The more I tried to tame it, the fiercer it became.
It retreated, only to retrogress wildly,
Traversing all the boundaries I inscribed for it.

I was drowning under its colossus,
and I guess, never called for help.
Maybe I needed no saving.
It sucked on the hope I had, but without it,
There wouldn't be any, to begin with.

I had befriended it lately
As it promised an adventure of a lifetime.
The pent-up furnace lying dormant for a long time
Seized the calm upon its release on its detonation.
Like I never imagined it to be.

Something that never happened before, happened!

Present Day

When the rest of the world was welcoming spring, Vancouver was still enthralled by the cold. The snow had thawed, making the greens visible, and the cars were now able to move swiftly without the tedious towing. But despite the cold, there was a warmth brewing inside me. My heart felt like a hot spring—it burned within my flimsy chest as flashes of memory from the day before intoxicated my mind. I had seen her after such a long time, and it still felt so surreal that she came to see me. I glanced at the clock on my wall; I noticed that light strands of cobwebs had begun to invade its surface. It was 8:30 AM, and there was sleep in my eyes, but my lips curved into a wide childish smile as the remnants of her comforting presence settled like stardust upon my body.

I ran my hands over the edge of my bed and caressed the sharp creases on the sheets–a temporary souvenir she had left me with when she sat there and talked to me. It was crazy how her tiniest gestures fascinated me even after all this time. The way she tucked the silky, loose strands of her hair behind her ears, the way her voice–confident and soft at the same time, echoed in a rhythmic tune, and how her hand gestures often mirrored her facial expressions; like when she would talk about something she was passionate about, I loved how her hands moved frantically about in the air, much like a dedicated choir conductor in a concert. A tingle ran through my right arm as I remembered the feeling of her hand brushing against mine as I passed her the PlayStation controller. She had accepted my invitation to play on my console despite her general disinterest in video games—which she only revealed before she left. And so, being the hopeless romantic that I was, I conjured up her visage once again in my mind. It wasn't hard to do so as I had done it a million times since I saw her for the first time. I tucked myself under my blanket for warmth and helplessly replayed the conversations I had with her yesterday.

"I should get going now. I have to wash my hair," she said, standing up from her spot.

"Going already? But we just started chatting!" I was unable to stop myself despite being hyper-aware of my actions. I wanted her to stay for some more time so that I could cherish her presence a little more. The twenty-something minutes of pure magic that I got to talk to her after our game made the rest of my life seem dull and mundane. But she always had this urgency about her. Like she would miss out on something pivotal in life if she stayed in one place for too long. That, I figured, was the tragedy of us. She didn't know how to stay; I didn't know how to hold on tightly unto things so they won't slip past my hands.

"Stay for a while, Maya," I said. She had no idea how many torturous moments it took for me to say those words out loud. I couldn't bring myself to tell her half of the things I wanted to. I just wanted to spend more time with her. Luckily, she decided to chat a little longer with me.

"Hmm... I listen to a podcast these days while taking a shower." She continued as she sipped on the coffee that I made for her.

"Oh really? I wonder what takes you so long that you have to listen to a podcast," I said, half chuckling.

"Washing my hair takes so much time, Gaurav. I have to apply shampoo thoroughly, rinse it, go for a second round, then rinse it again. Then I apply conditioner, keep it for a few minutes while I scrub my feet, especially heels..." She went on to list every detail of her routine, and I listened with close attention like it was the most encaptivating conversation ever; at least to me, it was. It wasn't every day that I got to see her talk so casually.

"What do you use for your hair and body?" She asked abruptly, pulling me out of the spell her voice cast upon me.

"Oh! Me?" I paused for a while, "I use Irish Spring soap." I said, becoming conscious of my answer.

"And for your hair?" She asked.

"Umm... same soap," I answered with a muffled voice. I could almost sense her judging me for my fourteen-year-old hygiene habits.

"You won't realize it right away, but skincare and haircare are important. If you start now, you will be able to see its good long-term effects on your body." She stared at my face for what felt like probably a few seconds but felt like an eternity to me. Perhaps she was assessing the extent of damage my skin had endured and the possibility of fixing it.

"You seem stressed. Working too hard, maybe?" She asked. Her words got me off-guard. There was a gentleness to her words that I yearned for. I didn't answer right away. I couldn't. The fact was that I had no idea where my life was headed. Ever since I moved to this city, I had been slightly lost. There was a subtle ache looming over me when she asked me that question.

"I'm okay, Maya," I said.

"You have Netflix and Apple TV+ on this PS5?" She asked, surprised, breaking the awkwardness I had displayed seconds ago. Then we proceeded to talk about a couple of movies we liked and disliked. I tried my best to stay in the moment with her. I knew there was no guarantee of her agreeing to come to see me again. That's just how things were.

"There is this series called Servant. I watched it twice already because it's so good. The main lead reminds me of you. Especially her voice, it sounds a lot like yours," I said in one breath, immediately regretting what I had just said.

She looked sideways, away from my gaze for a moment, looking slightly surprised by my comment.

"Hmm… I don't like how I sound." She confessed softly.

Then she stood up to go to my balcony to take a final glimpse of the view outside my newly rented high-rise apartment on the 39th floor. She had wanted to see it ever since I first shifted here. A few minutes later, she picked up her car keys bidding me goodbye as she left. I couldn't make her stay any longer. I failed to reach her once again.

It wasn't until 9:00 AM that I forced myself out of my bed and made my way towards the bathroom sink. I looked at myself in the mirror. She was right. I looked tired. Dark circles were sagging under my eyes, and I looked slightly older now.

Why am I like this? Why are these feelings about her still intact? You, Gaurav, had your life together for a good 24 years. You had a plan, and you stuck to it. Three years? You could have invested your time in something more productive—learned about crypto or the stock market or something. Or you could have worked towards a Ph.D., or hell, you could have learned a new language. But you chose to fall in love instead. The voice in my head bullied me.

I splashed my face with cold water, and I stood still in front of the mirror, watching drops of water slowly dripping down my chin.

Life was so much meaningful when I was younger. I was so much more than this lifeless figure staring back at me from the mirror's end. I excelled in my studies when I was younger, so people often used to tell me that I had inspired them to work harder. I figured that if those same people were to see me now, they would regret ever getting inspired by me. Because right now, I would just sit on my bed or the chair or stand in front of the mirror like a lifeless tree, waiting for some kind of inspiration to come to me or some inkling of motivation to push me forward.

I opened up a journal that she gifted me on Christmas few years ago. For a few seconds I just stared blankly at the ruled pages. Seconds turned into minutes. I took a deep breath and started scribbling, hoping it would lead me to my solace.

~~*~~

When it all Started

A two-story house with chestnut-brown walls, taupe beams, and a grilled balcony stood gallantly in front of a flourishing garden. On either side of its porch, the squared glass windows overlooked a cemetery. Its chic, rolled-up window blinds baited my eyes into fixating on that particular room. A soft, comforting light emanated from the window, putting even the last remnants of the warm sun rays in the dusky sky to shame. Inside the room was a girl with long hair that flowed straight down her back. I didn't realize I was staring. I stared long enough to realize that it wasn't my friend Lalita.

Who is she? I wondered. Well, tonight is Lalita's mother, Mrs. Caul's birthday party, so obviously there must be lots of friends and family coming over. What's the big deal? I wondered. But something about that figure inside that room arrested me. I could hear the endless echoey chatter from inside the house I was supposed to enter from a near distance. But instead of going in, there I was, looking up at the one sitting upstairs. I was never the type to stalk anyone. It was just that momentary impulse that made me stop and stare. I wasn't close enough to make out the color of her eyes or the texture of her skin, but close enough to see that she was a beautiful woman.

She was sitting at her desk, staring blankly at her laptop screen and biting her pursed lips, oblivious to my encaptivated gaze. She might have been working or studying or just surfing the web, or perhaps Googling: 'How to ward off a creepy stalker!' I cringed at the sudden realization of how pathetic I must have looked if anyone saw me staring at her from a distance. The sun was melting into the horizon at the backdrop of her illuminated room. For a moment, when the tiny ball of yellow light touched the edge of the roof, its rays dispersed into the atmosphere—blinding my eyes the way fireworks do. That was when I heard my roommate Kev's voice from the front door. I had almost completely forgotten about his presence and that he had been walking ahead of me all those times before I stopped abruptly. As expected, he blasted his voice in the manner of an announcement that he had arrived for the party. Before I rushed to catch up with him, I stole one last glance at the girl upstairs. I froze. She was looking at me from where she stood. Our eyes met for the first time.

Fuck! She caught me. Walk straight ahead, Gaurav! Like nothing happened. I felt my blood rushing to my cheeks.

"Kev, wait up!" I called out, walking towards the front door.

At least now, I had two valid reasons to hurry inside the house—one, the desperation to hide my embarrassment from her, and two, a genuine curiosity to know who she was. Either way, she was a vital conjunct serving both my purposes that night.

I bravely pushed on the front door standing ajar, and once I saw what was inside, I lost all my courage as quickly as I had mustered it.

THE OCEAN OF STRANGE NEW FACES AT THE PARTY OVERWHELMED ME.

~~*~~

Flashback - Early days of college

The campus roared with chaos, having awoken from its month-long December slumber. The first day in college was daunting. I flitted my eyes from one student to another. It was an utmost urgency that I had to find someone to share a rental suite with—a basement, to be precise; because I definitely couldn't afford a high-rise apartment, even if I wanted one badly. My nerves were all over the place that day. I didn't know a single soul in that desolate space filled with people. *"Come on. You got this, Gaurav,"* I whispered to myself. In my desperate attempt to get myself familiar with the basic geography of the campus, I had spent almost two hours wandering like a lost soul, after which my stomach started to twist horribly with a sudden bang of hunger. I quickly ran to get lunch.

At lunch, it was a complete chance that I happened to sit next to a guy who looked just as lonely as me, but not for the same reasons. He kept staring at his food like he was about to make the biggest decision of his life. I could see him tremble slightly. There were trickles of sweat on his nose and his forehead. I was a little worried about this man at that point, but I continued to observe him from my peripheral vision. I wondered if he had noticed me sitting right next to him. His tight grip on the cutlery turned his knuckles white, and the tension on his fat, red face intensified as he proceeded to take the meat chunks out of his plate with his fork and transferred them to an empty plate near his main dish, which he then covered with a piece of tissue. I finally understood the poor man's struggle. He proceeded to devour his meatless lunch with deep breaths, indicating that he felt calmer now that he was able to toss the meat away from his sight. The man just went through whole mental torture. I declared him a hero there and then.

"Planning on going vegetarian, huh?" I asked breezily while taking a bite of my veggie burrito, grabbing his attention. I wouldn't usually start any conversation with a stranger. But there was something about this man sitting next to me that radiated an aura of comfort—as though I could trust him completely. That was quite new to me.

"Have anything better to suggest, buddy?" He said with a mouthful, pointing at his round belly.

"Yeah, cut your head off. That's 20 unwanted pounds right there." I raised a smug smile.

Shit. Is that even a thing to say to a person you've just met!

"Bwa-ha-ha, nice one!" He said as his beefy body plumped up and down, laughing boisterously.

"My name is Kev. Nice to meet you!" He added in a friendly tone.

"I am Gaurav. Nice to meet you too! So, you rent nearby, Kev?" My eyes lit up with hope as soon as I asked him.

"I do. But it's complicated." He said, rolling his eyes.

"Really? Why? What happened?" I enquired nosily.

"Well, the thing is that my parents have some friends in the city, and I'm living with them until I can find a place of my own." He said as he slurped his cola generously.

"Oh, that seems cool," I said. We chatted for a while about the subjects we majored in and some other general stuff about each other.

I was a little bummed. Kev looked like a good prospect for me. His being almost vegetarian was already a significant upgrade from living with my interim flatmate, who couldn't go a meal without meat. This, topped with him being a psychology major who not only understood but also responded well to my twisted and often very awkward sense of humor with his natural, easy-going sarcasm, quickly made him the ideal person for a flatmate. I could at least try asking him—he seems pretty chill about things, I thought. But before I could even open my mouth to ask him, Kev banged his fists excitedly on the table, making me jump up from my seat.

"Hey Gaurav, we could live together if you haven't found a place yet!"

I could never understand the world of extroverts. It just took him two seconds to declare such an idea, while I was there dithering about whether I should even bring up the idea. But I was happy that people like Kev existed. They made things easier for introverts like me. I finally felt relaxed.

"Absolutely, why not!" I exclaimed as though I had never thought of that idea before. Sheesh. I could pretend well.

~~*~~

While I buried my face in my laptop screen, busy trying to find some kind of a job that could help pay for the rent that Kev and I were supposed to hunt for together, Kev was busy blabbering about his life in India, his plans in Canada, and an overwhelming number of unnecessary details that almost completely escaped my attention. A couple of days had passed since we met at the lunch table and decided to become roommates. He told me about his hosts—Mrs. Caul and her daughters and how they lived in a house built across from a cemetery. I was shocked at first. To live near a cemetery seemed unusually brave.

Was it an antiquated house? Or perhaps, an inherited property? I thought to myself. *Or was it avant-garde?* Nonetheless, it had to be huge like the ones we see in movies! Undoubtedly, the idea of a house near a cemetery does have a peculiar effect on one's imagination and curiosity. An air of mystery clouded my brain at the thought of the house. I had to see it for myself.

~~*~~

We knocked on a grand white door. Its central panel was embellished with gold paint. If the gaudy gold paint wasn't indication enough, a maroon Swastik hanging just above the doorbell convinced me that the residents were Indian. I rang the doorbell, and a commanding yet polite voice called out, "Who is it?"

I felt very nervous suddenly. I could never get used to that debilitating feeling of meeting a stranger for the first time.

The door was answered by a neatly-dressed woman in her fifties, who I assumed was Mrs. Caul. The slightest hints of grey in her hair betrayed her otherwise youthful face. Her face had the perfect amalgamation of motherly warmth and that natural commanding sternness often found in Indian mothers.

She smiled at Kev, "Hi beta, come on in!"

"Auntie, this is Gaurav, the friend I'm going to be moving in with. He's also from Delhi, just like you."

"Namaste, auntie! Very nice to meet you." I said, disguising my angst with a mask of confidence.

"Oh! Namaste!" She responded cheerfully. "You're from Delhi? We have much to talk about then Gaurav," she flashed the sweetest smile at me. Her wrinkles appeared prominently at the corner of her eyes when she did that. So, I figured it was genuine.

She quickly asked me about my parents, how I was adapting to the new culture away from India, and if I had made other friends besides Kev.

"No, Auntie. Only Kev. At least for now. Ha-ha." I said, finishing off with the most artificial laugh.

Gosh, that was awful. She must have seen right through that one. It's obvious that I'm not going to be making new friends that easily. I just got fortunate with Kev.

"That's okay, Beta—no need to rush. You'll meet the right people at the right time for sure," she flashed that smile again.

I don't know what it was about her, but she radiated a familiar warmth that I initially experienced when I met Kev for the first time. There was a certain level of comfort when I talked to them. They did not overwhelm me. They would just take me into the conversation, one step at a time. With Kev, there was that instant playful connection, and now with Mrs. Caul, it was more of that motherly aspect that calmed me in an instant. There is a difference in my demeanor when the other person opens up well to me first in our initial encounter. I immediately return the favor. But if the other person is someone like me, quiet and awkward, the room would most definitely be utterly cold and silent. I'm sure of that, at least.

"Let's chat over some tea! Give me a moment," Mrs. Caul said before she went into the kitchen. I quickly followed her to lend her a hand. We talked further while we waited for the water to boil. She told me about her Punjabi roots, her two daughters (who weren't home that evening), about

Kev too, of course, whose company she really enjoyed, and her absolute love for family gatherings and similar social activities like such. I told her about how she reminded me of my mom back at home, and she seemed to be really touched by it. "Oh Beta, I know you must miss her a lot." She said with a sigh as she tilted her head slightly.

"So, where are you kids planning to live?" She inquired in a more serious tone. It turns out that Kev had already discussed our plans with her the previous day.

"We're looking for a basement flat to rent, preferably closer to college Auntie," Kev said.
She thought for a while.

"You guys should try looking for flats on Fraser Street. It isn't far from here, it's close to your college and has many Indian stores. I'll give you some contacts."

"That sounds wonderful!" I was a bit relieved. She handed us the contacts before we left.

"Thank you, Auntie! We'll let you know how the hunt goes." Kev shouted from the front door exit.

"Bye, Beta. Good luck!" She smiled and slowly shut the door behind us.
The golden glimmer of the evening started to fade into an expanse of dark shadows as we walked back to catch our taxis.

~~*~~

The next day, we took Mrs. Caul's advice and wandered around Fraser Street with a bunch of contact info in our hands, also taking the liberty to knock on random doors, just in case we run into some sheer luck. Most of the flats had already been occupied, and the ones available were abysmal-musty basements, with damp walls, mold, infestations. Finding a suitable flat seemed like an impossible task.

Soon it became dark, and we hadn't managed to find a single basement that could be classified as a passable living space. Tired from all the walking and hustling, we had almost given up hope when we happened to come across a basement that was... well... livable. It didn't have a laundry room, but the lack of any mold or leakage made up for it, and the rent was comparatively more affordable. I cloaked my excitement in hopes of negotiating the rent, but the negotiation never happened. We left contented with what we had managed to procure that day, assuring the landlord that we would return with the deposit as soon as possible. We saw that there was a laundry shop just nearby while we crossed the street and felt utterly relieved at the sight of it.

The thrill of having a place that I could call my own kept me up all night. Well, of course, there was Kev, but the idea of being almost an adult was exciting. I spent the entire night budgeting my expenses and preparing a list of items we would need for our new flat. I closed my eyes and felt my heart beating restlessly. Will I be alright out here? Will I get a part-time job soon? Living by myself was going to be a new chapter in my otherwise uneventful life.

~~*~~

The week after, on a particularly cold evening, I got ready to leave for my new rental. I bid farewell to my flatmate and thanked him for introducing me to the international aisle at Walmart. It had been a lifesaver. I had relished all the Indian cuisines from that section. It was a constant reminder of home for me. I often called my mom or brother over the phone whenever I ate there. He helped me take my luggage outside, where I spotted Kev and Mrs. Caul waiting for me in an SUV with the headlights on. I rushed towards them with my bags to avoid the chill of winter that was biting into my skin and numbing my sense of smell. I loaded my luggage in the back of the car frantically and sighed in comfort as the warmth inside the car enveloped me like a woolen blanket. I greeted Mrs. Caul as I put on my seatbelt.

"How have you been? How is college Beta?" She asked inquisitively.

"The week went by so quickly, Auntie," I said, rubbing my hands together.

"Really? What kept you so busy?"

"Oh well, you know... applying for documents, searching for a part-time job, college assignments, rental hunting... as you know. Other than that, I've just been inside the room." I heard my voice fading as I realized how uninteresting and tedious my week had been.

"Wow, man. You've had such a fun week! Just like you." Kev interjected, giving me a sarcastic chuckle through the rearview mirror. He had tried to take me out somewhere a few days ago to meet a few of his other friends, but I had refused. I continued chatting with Mrs. Caul ignoring his tease.

After we arrived, Mrs. Caul, like the Punjabi mother she is, took the liberty of thoroughly inspecting the apartment and subjecting the landlord to a hundred different questions. Once she approved of the basement, to our relief, we handed over the rent to the landlord, who left immediately after receiving his share. Then, Mrs. Caul went into her zone of motherly instincts and began lecturing us as though we were little boys. I saw that she could be stern when she had to. She reminded me of my mother at times.

"Now that you have your own place, you better keep it clean," she said in a commanding tone looking at Kev. I've seen how messy he could be. No wonder she had to remind him.

"Yes, Auntie," Kev assured. Perhaps he has a history of not having the best hygiene practices in their house, I thought. Mrs. Caul then turned to me and said, "You shouldn't rely on his cleaning, Gaurav. He thinks cleaning means spraying Febreze on everything." She chuckled at the last words of the sentence.

"Oh, no! You're supposed to use Colin for glass surfaces, buddy." I said, returning him the look he gave me on the rear-view mirror on our way to the rental.

"You boys," Mrs. Caul said, half sighing, half laughing.

"Cleaning is much more than spraying Febreze..." and then turning to my side, she continued, "or Colin on glass surfaces."

Kev and I lowered our gazes like kids being reprimanded for stealing candy.

"Make a schedule. Start by making your bed right after you get up..." she walked towards the bathroom, "Take responsibility for cleaning the kitchen and bathroom twice every week. Pick your days and stick to them. Okay?" She asked, staring at both of us from a distance.

"Yes," I said, and Kev nodded in affirmation.

"You can call me if you need any help. I will be visiting soon, and the house better not be in shambles." She said while walking towards the door.

"It won't be, I promise! Thank you for your help, Mrs. Caul." I expressed my gratitude.

"You are welcome, Gaurav. Call me if you need me. Take care!"

~~*~~

The Meet

I was in the middle of shopping for some appliances for our new flat when my phone rang.

"Hi, Mrs. Caul!" I was surprised at the tone of my voice. Mrs. Caul seemed to have grown on me, and it was hard not to feel right at home with her.

"Hi beta! I just wanted to let you know that my daughter wanted to see Kev's new flat and meet his new flatmate. So, I was wondering if today would be a good time?" I was looking forward to spending a peaceful weekend on my couch watching television, and entertaining a stranger was the last thing I wanted to do. But instead, I replied, "Sure! I'll be home in fifteen minutes, and Kev is already there." I didn't have it in me to refuse Mrs. Caul.

"Well, okay then. I'll tell Lalita to come over in half an hour or so," and she hung up.

Why did she want to see our basement? What would we even talk about? Kev knows her already, and I'm going to be the awkward, silent one. I suddenly remembered that the flat hadn't been cleaned in a while and immediately called Kev. "Kev! Mrs. Caul just told me that one of her daughters was coming over. Could you please clean it up a little?"

"Daughter? Which one? Lalita?"

"Yeah, just please make sure the flat is clean." I really hoped that Kev would clean this one time. I had a particular itch and anxiety about first impressions, especially with girls. I rushed home, hoping to arrive before Lalita did, so I could do the cleaning that I was sure my flatmate wouldn't do despite me specifically instructing him to do so. I started mentally preparing myself for different scenarios and conversations, which didn't amount to much because all I knew about her was that she taught in a secondary school.

When I arrived at a surprisingly clean home, the relief that I felt was only short-lived. Seconds later, the doorbell rang, and I gathered all the courage I had to answer it, but Kev beat me to it as he excitedly rushed past me to greet her.

"Hey, shorty!" Kev grinned at her as she playfully punched him in the shoulder. They laughed and hugged each other, making me feel even more out of place. I had forgotten entirely that Kev had lived with them for a while now. Of course, they are close.

"Hello, Gaurav, nice to meet you finally!" Lalita said as she came inside and shook my hands.

"Nice to meet you too." I fumbled.

"Mom talks about you a lot." She added, laughing.

"Oh... does she? Okay." What was I supposed to say to that! That phrase could mean anything.

Lalita, however, not picking up on my nervousness, continued as she looked around the flat, "I can see why the flat looks great! And I've lived with Kev long enough to know that he isn't capable of this."

"Hey! FYI, I was the one who cleaned all of this!"

Lalita and I laughed at his pouty face, which eased the tension slightly but not enough for me to begin a conversation with her. She had a confident charm about her. I saw hints of Mrs. Caul's friendly demeanor when she teased Kev.

"By the way, what about your Lil sis?" Kev asked.

"Oh, she is out of the city for a while. She hardly stays home. That girl." She said.

We sat down on the couch as Kev insisted on being the one getting us some Frooti (a popular Indian mango drink that I was surprised and relieved to find in Canada) from the kitchen, leaving me alone with Lalita. Suddenly it was quiet. I didn't know what was so complicated about pouring some damn juice into a couple of glasses that Kev had to take ages to get out of the kitchen. I was pretty sure he was doing it on purpose, to get me to talk. The awkwardness hung heavy above us as I tapped my fingers on my knees, trying to come up with some casual conversation starters.

"So, how is college?" She broke the silence first.

"It's going good… great! Thanks for asking."
The heck was that! Why'd you have to be so formal about it? At least elaborate, Gaurav.

"Cool. How do you like your job at the gas station?"

How did she even know about this!

"Oh…well…I…I don't like it, of course, but it pays for my expenses, so…"

"I know, right…" she said with a hint of pity in her eyes.

"Any career plans for later?"

Where is Kev? What's taking him so long? I need him to come and take over this conversation before I make a fool out of myself.

"Yeah, law enforcement. I want to…"

"Here's the world's best drink ever…" Kev finally arrived at the dreadful scene. What took you so long, loser?

The moment he arrived, Lalita turned her attention towards him (to my relief).

I sipped on the Frooti, slowly and delicately, like a well-mannered child while Lalita and Kev bickered, earning a laugh out of me now and then. I gradually eased into their conversation, chipping in with my jabs at Kev, who went on a rant on how Lalita had turned his flatmate against him. They had this natural chemistry about them. I envied them. Why was I always so tensed up when I met people? Why do I want to be left alone most of the time? Even while I was watching them tease each other and smiling at them, I felt the urge to go to my room and sink into my mattress. I felt drained after my long day of shopping.

As Kev cleared up the glasses, Lalita sensing my discomfort took it upon herself to keep the conversation going.

She narrated funny stories about her and Kev and allowed me the luxury to sit and listen to her comfortably. I began to enjoy her company as we exchanged some laughter. No wonder Kev and her got along well. They radiated the same energy. Lalita, with her confidence and charm, turned what I thought would be a dull evening into a well-treasured memory.

~~*~~

*Vacations take the world away from home.
I'll fly home for it.*

College was over, and I wanted to visit Delhi before a full-time job would bind me. I traveled by train a lot in India, where a typical journey took a minimum of twenty hours, that is, if the train ran on the schedule, of course. Spending half that time on a plane was peanuts for me, or at least that's what I thought.

I was trying to enjoy some in-flight movies—a sure-shot way to pass the time quickly in a 14-hour Economy. Here the long Bollywood movies came to my rescue especially. I was visiting home after a long time. College life had been stressful, and now I was finally going to see my folks. I wanted to enjoy my movie during the long, dreadful flight. But unfortunately, as though all the forces in the universe were working against me, for some reason, the girl next to me wished to take a stroll and use the lavatory every thirty damn minutes! I was sitting towards the aisle. What a curse! Her constant interruption of my peace resembled that annoying kid on the block whose incessant screams annoyed the whole of the neighborhood. You begin to hate the peace snatcher—his voice practically. Here, this girl could not stay seated. I had not slept well the previous night because of the perpetual anticipation of going back home and seeing my family after so long.

Again, she slid right past me smiling, which I found annoying for a very profound reason. I smiled back forcefully.

I thought she was settled. I put on my headphones for the twentieth time when the air hostess approached my seat.

"How can I help you, Ma'am?"

"Can I have some more soda?" She asked.

I subtly sneered at her. *More soda? Does she realize what she is asking for? She's going to start her pee breaks again!*

I wish I could have said something to her or maybe gotten my seat exchanged or something, but she wasn't even the real clown of the class. Passengers were strolling in the plane's aisle like in some park. What are they even on! I thought. I could see the concern and frustration oozing out of the hostess. Some stretched their arms and legs, unbothered by the awkwardness they were creating for their fellow passengers. Then another breed took this game on a whole new level as they did sit-ups mid-flight. I closed my eyes, hoping to land soon before succumbing to the lunatic haywire all around me. I kept consoling myself that I was flying with a tribe of baboons. I would have unhesitatingly gone for a premium economy. But this was all I could afford with my hard-earned money made from filling gas and washing windshields in wasted hopes of making tips. As thoughts about the general mayhem and better ways of spending my hard-earned CADs ran through my mind, I didn't realize when I began to doze off.

~~*~~

But as expected, just minutes after my coveted journey to my dreamland, a screeching sound pierced through my ears. My red-shot eyes split open to the commotion on board. People were searching for their footwear in the dark and dragging bags from under their seats and the cabinets above, while others were trying to get a hold of their crying kids. All that drama just so that they can save a spot in the line soaring near the washrooms, like devotees lining up to enter a shrine. The remaining duration of the flight turned washrooms into the frequent flyers' Mecca; believers had to go offer their prayers before they died. My head began to feel heavy with thoughts, plus the air pressure in my ears wasn't helping either. I imagined myself going up to the speakers and screaming my lungs out.

Why do all of you have to take a piss at the exact same time!? What were you doing for the past fourteen fucking hours? Can't you just wait for a few more minutes? There are a lot more washrooms at the airport. And ladies, who are you getting ready and applying all that make-up for at three in the morning? Immigration agents? Taxi drivers? Or the family members waiting outside the arrivals, standing among a million other people in thirty degrees Celsius heat, probably sweating more water than you drank in this whole flight? What's wrong with you people?

38

I just could not shut my brain off. My ears began to hurt because I had not removed my headphones for God knew how long. I turned my head away, trying to ignore the line for a minute and then peeking at it the next. It was getting longer to the point that there was now a person or two worth of distance between it and my seat. I lost my ease as I imagined someone hovering over my head all the time. It was like a game of hide-and-seek for me, but only worse, since I knew I was going to be peek-a-booed soon when I didn't even want to play! I thought I was going nuts, but more crazy stuff was yet to happen.

A finger jabbed me on my shoulder, taking my attention away from the line and towards my "chivalrous" co-passenger, "Excuse me! Can I ask you for a quick favor?" Quick favor? Are you serious right now? NO!

"Sure. What is it?" I replied. I gave her a dead expression. I failed miserably to hide the sarcasm practically dripping from my tone.

She gave me a quick frenzied look, "Could you please…" pointing her finger upward, "bring my bag down?"

My nerves were triggered yet again. I could not believe the sheer lack of decency of the people around me.

"We still have some time. I'll help you when we land?" I tried to sound as polite as possible.

"No, I wanted to get something from it before we landed so I could use the washroom. Please…?"

I hope you don't find what you need in your bag.

"Oh, alright then," I said as I stood up.

I dragged her bag down, putting it on my seat. I was still standing until madam took out a plethora of make-up products, after which I had to put it back up.

The landing was like the calm before the storm. Tremors shook the floor as soon as the seatbelt signs went off. People tried getting off all at once, but nobody could move because of the clutter they had caused. Luggage fell on heads, feet were stepped upon, kids went crazy wild, and their parents... wilder. A million cell phones rang. Some were shouting... no actually, most were shouting because a hell lot of that occurred. There was so much noise that it muffled the pilot's announcement. I was almost sure I heard a 'fuck you all' before he hung up, or that could have been just me. Amidst all this hullabaloo, an air hostess stood across the section near the door, folding her hands in a namaste and watching all those animals jumping around. Our eyes met, and we held our gaze for a few moments, making everything else invisible. She had a weird half-angry, half-smiling kind of a face. 'Obviously, she has had enough of the circus show as well,' I thought and managed to give her a pitiful smile from where I was seated. She smiled back at me, and I thought about how she was the only normal human besides me on that flight.

~~*~~

Apart from my co-passengers scattered all over the baggage hall and washrooms (surprising since they seemed a little too eager to use the washrooms specifically on the plane), the airport wasn't busy. I connected my phone to the Wi-Fi and received a message on WhatsApp from my brother saying he wouldn't be able to pick me up from the airport as our car, which had been acting strangely for the past few months, had broken down. I pointlessly replied that I would take a taxi instead. Indeed, there was nothing else in the universe that was capable of disappointing me after all the ruckus I had experienced in that godawful flight. Hundreds of people, if not thousands, were gathered outside the airport, cheering at the sight of whoever they were there for—clapping, whistling, hooting, hugging, and crying. Some put garlands around the necks of their dear ones. There was too much emotion, heat, and noise. I saw people wiping tears from their eyes. Some of them held hands and talked about how much they had missed each other. The commotion slowly turned into an emotional conclusion for me. I was home, whatever that word meant. I felt the thickness in the air around me. I was finally in Delhi. The city of my boyhood ventures.

As I walked past the noisy crowd, I felt the weight of nostalgia tugging at my heartstrings, and I slowly walked towards the exit, leaving the ceremony of reunions behind me.

As I paced towards the taxi stand, someone pounced on me from behind and patted on my shoulder, "Gaurav!" I saw a familiar face running towards me with a bunch of minions behind him.

"Aman!!" I exclaimed as I hugged my brother and slapped his back. "Is Papa paying you to be my chauffeur for the day?" I laughed, stroking the fabric of the grey suit he was wearing.

"Aha-ha, no! I dressed up for you! You have absolutely no value for my brotherly love, do you?" He retorted with a mock huff. Next to him were my cousins with wide grins on their faces. I liked to believe that they were excited to see me and not just the gifts and souvenirs I had brought for them.

"How did all of you..." I started hugging them, "manage to come?"

"What do you mean?" Karan said.

"We got a nice big car, bro!" Aman exclaimed.

"Bwa-ha-ha…" They took me for a fool.

"You didn't have to take the trouble of coming all the way here to pick me up. I have only one bag with me. I'm so stupid. I forgot the one that had gifts for all of you." I bluffed.

"No way!!" They screamed, almost unanimously.

"You can't be serious!"

"I sacrificed my sleep for this!" One of the younger cousins complained.

Their foreheads furrowed for a moment but then quickly relaxed when I looked at them with a mischievous smile.

"Aiee…You got us!" They giggled at their own expense.

"Of course, I did, you selfish assholes." I burst out laughing, followed by theirs in unison. We walked towards the parking lot.

"We are even now!" I commented as I sat in the car. Aman took the wheel, and we cruised back home.

The sudden realization of being back in the capital city of India hit me when we got stuck in traffic for a whole hour. The ear-splitting honks and blares overwhelmed my senses. The pollution began to suffocate me. It dawned upon me how the refined lifestyles of the West had reduced my tolerance to the heat and pollution of Delhi, which was as natural as breathing for me when I was younger.

~~*~~

Three weeks into my vacation and I had met enough people who I wished I had never met. Being a foreign return with two degrees and a job that paid in dollars (though they had no idea about the odd temporary jobs I did), made me more than an eligible suitor for marriage. Every now and then, I was remembered by some long-forgotten relative who wondered what living in Canada was like. For them, it was a wonderland covered in snow, inhabited by the most exotic race of humans—the white people—a place where only the luckiest of people could go and settle. Little did they know that Canada often felt more Indian than India—the food, the people, the languages, the culture, and everything else in between could be so very Indian. I had encountered many fellow Indians in Canada over the lapse of three years.

Anyway, I didn't understand the logic of how one could become such a treasured candidate for marriage just because they have lived in the west. Clearly, some of my relatives seemed to believe that careless notion. In the end, it all came down to marriage, and the very thought of it brought shivers down my spine. I didn't get why people were so eager to settle. I have seen failed marriages everywhere I go, in Delhi while I was a boy and also in Canada. It's everywhere, and I had seen how devastating it could be. Besides, why should one marry without falling in love? I thought. From my boyhood days, I had nurtured this grand notion of finding "the one" when I grew up to be an adult. Perhaps it was the Bollywood movies that I watched too often and its embellishment on the idea of love that had seeped into my conscience. To me, love was a dream—distant yet achievable, but I kept escaping its clutches. I knew love bore challenges, and I would just be a child falling down this pit, the mayhem of thoughts, unable to recover from its distorting trance. I wanted it, but I wasn't ready for it. It felt too risky for me, like believing that a dream was real, and once

I would wake up from it, I'd be left devastated. Yet, despite this fear, whatever hope I've had as a child on finding my love, it still clung to me like a forgotten tattoo in my flesh. Maybe I just had to wait for the right moment? I thought. My endless paradox baffled me sometimes.

Clearly, you won't find her if you keep crawling back into your mental cave every time you meet someone new, Gaurav.

It's funny how I had this voice inside of me—always picking on me, providing pearls of wisdom for life. But I never listened.

My days back home felt rather slow and dreamy. I would go out occasionally to attune myself to the city of my childhood. Delhi felt like an old friend I had stopped contacting. It seemed to know me well, but it couldn't embrace me fully. Or perhaps, it was the other way around. Maybe it was me who had changed entirely while it remained as it was. I visited the book stores that had been my haven during high school. I crossed the streets flooded by rickshaws and autos. I repulsively inhaled the stench of the drainage oozing out near the sidewalks and stopped by a street stall to enjoy a cup of chai once in a while. I did all this to become one with the city, at least while I was there. Some days it welcomed me, and I was transported to the realm of my childhood memories where I knew its temperaments very well, just like the way I knew my mother's home-cooked meals. Other days, I was a complete stranger—like a tourist or an alien of sorts, trying to piece together a cultural puzzle of the city. I failed miserably at it and found myself feeling the same way I felt when I first stepped foot in the West's culture. I was lost, perpetually.

But like all good things, my holidays came to an end. The last day saddened my family and brought my hopes for a non-dramatic departure crashing down. The theatricality of the event lurched in my mind as I departed. A motorcade of six cars and about twenty-five people came to bid me farewell at the airport. The crying faces made me wonder if those were tears of separation or a deep-rooted agony of not making it to the West.

Aman dropped me in our nice big car, a Chevrolet Spark, that now had empty back seats. It was fully packed and rocking with music when I arrived three weeks earlier. However, the ride back to the airport was silent, and an air of melancholy loomed above us. Maybe he wanted the ride to take longer so he could spend more time with me, just as I wanted to stay back for a longer period and spend more time with him and Delhi.

I saw the corner of his eyes sparkle as I waved him goodbye at the entrance gate.

My long-awaited graduation ceremony was scheduled for the day after I arrived in Vancouver. I had no idea what job I would get or if I had to move to another place. There was so much uncertainty about the next few weeks. I didn't want to keep thinking about the future, so I slept almost the entire flight, waking up only when the food got served. Eating helped me get my mind off the future and instead made me scrutinize trivial matters like the clamoring of the co-passengers and their kids, the shabby-looking host, and his tasteless food. All these thoughts had enthralled me, and in a minute, I felt the ruckus around me fading away like a sweet rhythmic lullaby.

~~*~~

Ceremonial Frenzy

"What a day!" I said as I pushed through the crowd gathered at the airport. Luckily, I found a taxi to drop me at my location. As the cab passed through the suburbs, I almost felt like I was in a different city altogether, a utopia of my own, oblivious to what it will offer me in the near future.

Getting out of the taxi, I sighed, looking at my basement. Even before I dragged my suitcase to my room, Kev appeared in front of me, grinning.

"Welcome back, my Desi friend! How did the Delhi air treat you?"

"Very well, Kev. Very well."

He continued asking many random questions without letting me answer them properly.

"Hey bro, I have no idea what to wear for the graduation ceremony. I have the blue suit and the grey blazer and…" He went on about his attire.
It was easy for me, though. I had only one neatly-ironed suit for the occasion.

The same evening, someone rang the doorbell, and I dragged my jet-lagged self to the door. "Oh… Please come in!" I stuttered surprisedly at my landlord. When did I become important enough for the landlord to visit me?

"How are things in the apartment?" He asked.

"Great, sir! Everything seems to be fine. Is there a problem?"

"Now that the lease is coming to an end, I was thinking of increasing the rent," he said tentatively, expecting some resistance from me. But to his surprise and mine, I gave him a hopeless look and agreed. I was already exhausted from the flight and struggling to adjust to the time difference. I had no energy to fight any bullshit. In hindsight, I should have let Kev say something, but that ship had already sailed. I knocked myself out the moment I laid my head on my pillow.

~~*~~

I could barely open my eyes, wanting to go back to sleep for a hundred more years. I would have skipped the ceremony if it wasn't for my grandma. But her excitement to see me in my graduation gown, even if it was in the picture, kept me from letting her down. I recalled how a childlike joy emanated from her wrinkled face as she spoke about how amazing it could have been if she could attend my graduation day, oblivious to my absolute abhorrence for ceremonies such as these. It made me uncomfortable and tense. I wasn't keen on attending a function where five hundred students would come with their family and friends, chit-chatting and posing for a million photos and selfies like it would be their last day on earth. Shivers spiked my spine at the thought of the ceremony hall, crammed with the so-called leaders of tomorrow. As the idea grew heavier with every passing second, I felt myself shrinking into nothingness—withering into a small insignificant thing in a big world.

Regardless of my thoughts, Graduation Day finally arrived at our front doors. Kev and I decided to suit up nicely for the occasion. While I was struggling with my tie and maintaining the crease of my blazer, Kev entered, showing off his expensive and well-ironed formal shirt and trousers. His shoes shone as bright as his future, and he wore an old G Shock watch. He looked as confident as ever.

I somehow managed to get dressed, but the thought of riding a packed bus in that attire made us laugh uncomfortably.

"We have to wear this and travel in a bus like high school students on a field trip? We are going to look so ridiculous," Kev voiced out with concern.

We shut the door behind our backs and headed out. Kev could barely look through my well-groomed face. A socializer like him couldn't fathom the anxiousness of an introvert who dreaded the very thought of being a part of a social gathering.

I tried to push these thoughts away and started walking towards the bus stop. As I proceeded, I felt a strange heaviness settling in my soul. I momentarily stopped and almost retreated like a lost soldier to take a final look at my peaceful haven. I wanted to go back and shut myself in my room for the rest of the day, but I was suddenly reminded of Mrs. Caul. She had called me early in the morning to tell me that she would be present in the crowd to cheer for both Kev and me when we received our certificates. How could I disappoint her? It felt like centuries ago since I last saw her and had a chit-chat. She would most definitely be looking forward to seeing me too. I had no choice but to go. The college campus was a different place that day—much grander and decorated in every nook and corner. I saw Mrs. Caul standing in the parking lot. We joyfully exchanged our mutual enthusiasm on meeting after a long gap, after which I escorted her to the welcome area where guests stayed until the graduates spruced up in their suit and gown. It was a bright summer morning, and I could feel the scorching heat of the sun as I felt my white shirt getting soaked in sweat under the weight of my uncontrolled sweat glands. Despite being in an air-conditioned hall, the heat kept encroaching my brain. I looked like a clown in the gown—a stage-fearing, attention-phobic clown who knew his show would be a disaster. On the other hand, Kev stood on the other side of the hall cracking jokes with a group of classmates about how the ceremony felt like some 'coming of age' ritual.

The hall was crowded with people who were constantly engaged in endless chatter. The variation in their voices blustered in unison, resulting in a strange musical cacophony, making the hall more chaotic each passing minute. It began to feel a lot like the disarray during my flight to Delhi.

The opening speech commenced. The principal broke out into charismatic prose on how special the occasion was for the institution. He ran on for about a good half hour. Nobody, except some people in the front, seemed to take him seriously. The atmosphere around me began to melt into a blur, and I lost my focus on the program. I was sucked into a vacuum inside my head. It felt like I was high on something. Voices began to drop, and an eerie sense of calm settled in the hall. Then in a flash, I was back into the real world when the announcer started calling out the names of my classmates who were supposed to come and receive their well-deserved certificates and shake hands with the vice-chancellor.   I kept reminding myself to strictly follow and remember their steps to avoid creating an awkward scene and save myself from getting unwanted attention. That sounded simple enough. Just follow what the other students are doing before you, and you will be fine, Gaurav!

But I was going to prove myself wrong in a short while.

As they called Kev's name, everyone in my group began cheering. I followed the crowd and smiled at Kev as he glanced at me right before standing up. He was pretty popular among the crowd. Who wouldn't like him? As he walked on the stage, I saw Mrs. Caul slowly walk out of the aisle with her iPhone in her hand and click pictures of him from the side of the aisle. She waved at him so that he could pose properly for a picture. But it wasn't until the official photographer standing in the front center of the aisle signaled him that he got the perfect photo that Kev started walking off the stage showing off his hard-earned degree to Mrs. Caul, who responded to his confidence with a loud "Wooo!" and a series of quick camera clicks from her phone.

He had just walked a few steps from the stage when my name was called. As I walked towards the stage, my ears began heating up, and I suddenly felt like I was losing balance. The voices echoing in the hall just a second ago faded, and I felt a numbing sensation gradually steering my senses. As I climbed up the stairs, I felt a strong force holding me back, restraining any further movement. A sudden tap on my shoulder revived me, and I looked up to see my friend Kev standing right in front of me. He shook me and said, "Hey bro, where is your cap?" I realized the blunder I had made. As I looked back at my seat, I found my graduation cap sitting motionless as if silently mocking me. Fear paralyzed my senses. It was too embarrassing to turn around and get my hat. So, I ignored Kev's question and went on ahead.
Forget it, Gaurav! It's not like you will be denied your certificate just because of a silly hat!

Finally, I reached the spot where I would shake hands with the VC, but someone from the crowd shouted my name.

"Gaurav! Here buddy. Catch!" And my hat came flying towards me like a frisbee. Someone from the crowd had passed on my hat to the front row, and they managed to get it for me.

As much as I wanted to catch it, the nervousness that occupied my mind wouldn't let me. The hat slipped from my grip and dropped on the floor of the stage. An immediate reaction came from the crowd in the form of a swarm of laughter. I wanted it all to end so I could get off the stage as soon as possible, but it seemed like a never-ending fiasco. I somehow managed to pick up my hat and dusted it clean before placing it gently on my head, covered in sweat. My credentials were called out as I held my diploma in my hands, and I simultaneously shook hands with the VC.

"Many congratulations!" He said.

"Gaurave to you…I mean…congrats!"

"Sorry?" He said with an awkward laugh.

"I am so sorry. I mean…Thank you so much!"

"Face this way for the photo," he said, amplifying the embarrassment I was going through. For a moment, I felt a dense void feeding on my consciousness, leaving my body as nothing but an effigy as I stood still on the stage, struggling to smile for a photograph. I heard a loud and cheerful "Woooo!" from Mrs. Caul from a distance. I looked at her, and she quickly captured some pictures before I exit the stage.

That brief experience on the stage seemed like an endlessly haunting series of incidents. I plunged back in my seat and took off my hat, and started wiping the waterfall of sweat that had accumulated on my face. Kev nudged me and gave me a fist bump. "You looked pretty cool up there, buddy!" He said. What I had done was just a silly mistake for him, but for me, it felt like an entire mountain had been placed atop my body, for me to carry it for the rest of my life.

I passed a sigh of relief as I realized it was all over finally. I walked over to the aisle and thanked Mrs. Caul for attending the ceremony. Her over-enthusiastic self couldn't keep her from patting my back, and after congratulating Kev and me innumerable times, she invited us to a party at her house. It turns out it was her birthday.

"Oh, my goodness, Auntie. It's your birthday?" I felt guilty for not having prepared any gift for the sweet lady.

"Yes, Gaurav. It is. And I want both you and Kev to come over for a dinner party after you are done here, okay?"

The timing was just devastatingly perfect.

Why did it have to be tonight? I need some alone time to recover from today's trauma, Mrs. Caul. You have to let me off the hook, please! My mind roared underneath my calm demeanor.

I wished her and tried to make several excuses for avoiding the party, but if there was one thing I had learned about Mrs. Caul, it was that she never got tired of insisting when it came to social gatherings. Moreover, Kev had already promised our presence, and there was no option left but to attend the party. My mind grew dreary at the thought of another gathering, and all I could think of was retiring peacefully in my bed, away from all the humdrum, in a silent sanctuary of my own.

Mrs. Caul knew how shy I was around a crowd by then. So, she assured me that it was a small family get-together, but I had fallen for that before. Only after arriving at the scene you realize you are surrounded by uncountable people at what was supposed to be a small get-together. And by then, there is no going back because you are already deep within the pit with no way to climb out.

"See you tonight, Beta. I don't remember the last time you visited my place. It'll be a great reunion!"

She left in her SUV with a huge smile. How could I possibly betray that smile? I thought as I let out a deep sigh.

Another gathering with lots of people catching up with each other on their eventful lives... I would have no idea how to function like a normal human being with an ocean of faces coming at me all at the same time!

What if they ask me something on a topic I have no knowledge about? Or worse, what if they ask me about something I know a lot about? Whatever it is, they better not ask me about my plans for the future because I don't know, okay! What do I get Mrs. Caul for her birthday? What will I even wear—this suit? That would be too much for a birthday party. How about pajamas and a T-shirt to look a little more relaxed? But wouldn't that be a little too casual? It's a party, after all. Wait, how many people are going to be there exactly? 10, 20? Or a lot more than that? How am I going to greet them—individually or collectively? But I don't have to, right? I can just stand in a corner and wait for Kev. Why does he always seem so excited to go to a party full of new faces? No, wait…ugh. He probably knows most of the guests anyway. Does that mean I will have to pretend to participate in random conversations? Oh, how I despise that. Well, I only know two people there—Mrs. Caul and Lalita. I will tell Mrs. Caul that I am not feeling too well. Am I overthinking or just thinking? What day is it today? Wait, what does it have to do with the party? Ugh… I am overthinking! Can I just defuse my existence!?

I finally decided to wear some decent, comfortable clothes to the party and took out a well-ironed black shirt and a pair of blue jeans from my cupboard. I dressed up and waited for Kev, a man with a fashionable taste unlike me. He spent a considerable amount of time perfecting his attire, paying attention to every minor detail. I watched him groom himself into a perfect gentleman as he got ready for the party.

He finally wore his favorite perfume and said, "Let's go, mate." I responded with a tired nod, and we both left the house and started towards the bus stop. There was something uncanny about that evening, something that I had never noticed before. It was as if a strong hand was driving me towards my destiny. I felt I had no control for a second, and an incomprehensible force was at play, rendering me completely powerless. We took a bus to Metrotown and got off at Burnaby Central Park. Right across the road was the cemetery that I had tried to picture several times before, painting a vivid image of it in my mind. It was about a few minutes walk downhill to Mrs. Caul's house from the bus stop. As I followed Kev, walking on the trail beside the cemetery, I kept turning and looking back towards it, comparing the actual image to the one I had painted in my mind.

The cemetery spanned across a vast area of two blocks. It was a large expanse of land enveloped in lush green grass and tiny white blossoms that veiled the graves of the dead—a space shut out from the outside world, making it seem like a peaceful abode only for the deceased. The view of the cemetery made me feel a certain way. There is a reverential character about it. Something about it makes one ruminate and reflect. I watched as the shadows of the cemented tombstones stretched sideways. If you gazed at it long enough, it seemed to morph into the shadow not of the stones but the human lying underneath in eternal sleep, reaching out towards the green grass above the soil. From a distance, I could see a few people offering their prayers over the graves of their loved ones. They had large flower bouquets, differing in color—perhaps representing the shades of grief they had gone through. I looked around and saw that many of the tombstones had the luxury of being decorated with fresh flowers while still many had none. Or worst still, they had a single bouquet of fake flowers to guard its shadows in a fallacy of colorful permanence. My heart went out to them.

I saw an old caretaker gently sweep away the heaps of fallen leaves that had settled on the pathways. He looked like a guardian of some sort, serving as the reminder of life amid the desolate reality of death around him every day. As I watched him, the birds began to chirp in harmony—in a steady cadence, making the view in front of me a little less lonely. Moderate gusts of breeze carried the fresh smell of limestone, soil, and flowers to my nostrils, and it seemed to have a calming effect on me. It was only when Kev snapped at me in annoyance for not listening to a thing he had said to me that I sailed back to the taunting reality of going to a party. But then, I realized something fascinating. That the silent existence of the cemetery had shut my mind, even if for a moment, away from my anxious thoughts and fears. I felt a certain calm that I wished I could have possessed a little longer.

Kev had already moved ahead by a long measure, unable to wait for my slowed pace. I jogged lightly to try and catch up with him. As I strolled towards the house, I was suddenly distracted by a warm light coming from the large square windows at the top of the house. I stopped abruptly and glanced upwards. That was when I finally saw her.

The Sorcery

Continued from 'When it all Started'

I could feel my heart pounding as I closed the door behind me. The moment I entered, the people laughing and joking around took a break from their engagements and turned their heads towards me. They scrutinized the new individual that had entered for a few moments (which felt like an eternity for me) and went back to their conversations casually. I was still recovering from the embarrassment of being caught by the girl upstairs. I regretted standing outside for a long time like a directionless fool, staring at a lady.

Shit! And now I have to deal with a crowd? I screamed inside.

I was surprised when some of them smiled and waved at me, only to painfully realize that it was directed towards Kev, who was right in front of me. It seemed as though I had sold my soul to the God of embarrassment that day. Ever since the graduation ceremony stage fail, nothing seemed to go smoothly for me.

Do I greet everyone at once, or do I go up to them individually? While I was busy contemplating one of the most defining choices of my life at that moment, Kev had already greeted the guests individually with a "Hi, how are you!!" and had moved on to find a seat near the center of the room. He looked relaxed, too relaxed in my opinion, sitting like that with his chest out and his elbows on the arms on the couch. He almost looked like a nonchalant business tycoon. But then, that was just Kev. He was a natural crowd puller. I sometimes wondered what he got from being my friend. Someone like him would generally dislike people like me—who would rather stay away from people and parties.

Maybe it's not just me who has to put up with him. I guess he does so with me as well.

With Kev away from my side, I awkwardly smiled at two or three strangers who seemed to have noticed and waved at me. Mrs. Caul was nowhere to be seen. What about Lalita, then? My eyes darted in search of a familiar face.

It took me a few minutes to study the room and the atmosphere around me. Still, I gradually settled in by answering people's questions and thanking those congratulating me on earning my diploma. My eyes were now in search of that particular girl I saw upstairs. Was she still upstairs? What is she doing up there? Did she feel taunted by the party as well? I thought to myself.

I finally spotted Mrs. Caul coming out of the kitchen with a snack tray accompanied by that usual flashy smile. I immediately waved at her, wishing her again on the occasion of her birthday. She formally introduced me to everyone as Kev's friend. I wished she would have stopped at that, but she went on, "Gaurav is such a polite and lovely boy, everyone." I began to blush and avoided any form of eye contact. "He's from Delhi and studied at the same university as Kev. And that's about all the similarities between the two of them," she added jokingly.

"Excuse me? Auntie? Am I not sweet?" He responded. I could sense that the comment made Kev feel slightly jealous, but he joined in the laughter in a manner that the comment escaped everyone's attention. I was about to ask Mrs. Caul where Lalita was when she came out of the kitchen with the cake and rushed back in, only to return with another one. The next moment, Mrs. Caul announced for everyone to come to the table so that they could enjoy the cake she and Lalita had baked.

"Kev! Gaurav! Come here quick, will you?" Lalita called out as she waved at us. I went past the crowd and stood next to her.

"Everyone! As you can see, there are two large cakes," she said, pointing at the table.

"This one's for my mom's birthday celebration, and this one right here is for Kev and Gaurav." Kev and I looked at each in utter surprise.

"Yes, yes. The second cake is to celebrate your graduation day, my boys," Mrs. Caul clarified.

"It's eggless, by the way, Gaurav. No need to worry," Lalita said.

I looked at the cake Lalita had baked for us; it looked delicious and smelled even better with the pistachios and blueberry sprinkled on top.

I was surprised when she told me the cake was eggless and surprised even more still that she remembered I was a vegetarian.

"That's really sweet of you, Lalita. Thank you!"

I was touched by this kind gesture and resisted the urge to hug her because it was only the second time I met her, and I didn't want to cause her any discomfort. On the other hand, Kev went straight ahead and hugged both Mrs. Caul and Lalita, ending with a sneaky peck on Lalita's cheeks. She rolled her eyes with a playful smile. I noticed something different in her appearance but couldn't figure out exactly until a lady complimented her for her beautiful short hair. She really looked great that evening.

But something didn't sit right with me. I couldn't relax. I had an impending desire in my heart. I had half-expected the gorgeous young woman I had seen just before I entered to have made an entrance by now. I was still embarrassed that she had seen me standing there, though just for a few seconds. I didn't understand why all the other guests were in the room except her. Everyone was gathered around the cake, waiting for Mrs. Caul to blow the candles.

"Do you guys want candles on yours?" Lalita asked. I made a noncommittal shrug in response.

We had only been declared graduates. It hadn't changed much in my life. I still had a long way to go before I could truly celebrate. She then turned towards Kev, who excitedly grabbed two candles from her hand and lit them himself, making Lalita giggle. Mrs. Caul was about to blow out the candles when I don't know if desperation or courage made me interrupt her. In a quick and assertive voice, I said, "I hope everyone is here?" I couldn't believe it. Why would I suddenly care if everyone is there? I suddenly started to panic if anyone found it obvious that I had asked such a question. But despite all my useless rantings in my mind, my strategy worked.

Everyone started looking around the room, mentally calculating when Lalita suddenly let out a huge gasp and seemed to remember.

"Oh, Maya!" and she hastily ran upstairs. Mrs. Caul smiled at everyone and touched her forehead with her left hand. She giggled in embarrassment.

"My younger daughter is upstairs. She'll be here in a few seconds," she said guiltily. "Oh, Maya! Is she home, Auntie? Haha, that's a surprise!" Kev chuckled.

Only at that moment did I realize that Mrs. Caul had two daughters. Not just one. She had told me once during our first encounter, and so did Lalita when she came to meet Kev and me in our new rental. But it had been so long that the information had completely left the chambers of my brain. Besides, only Lalita would occasionally be there in the few times I had visited Mrs. Caul with Kev. And also, we never talked about family matters. It was always some other topic that governed our conversations. Maya. My head began to spin at the sudden connection of dots. I could not believe that the pretty woman I had wanted to get a glimpse of all evening was Lalita's younger sister. It made it worse for me that she had quite possibly seen me standing there like a fool facing her window.

So, her name is Maya. How nice! I wonder why she didn't come earlier? It's her mom's birthday. Hmm…that's odd. Is she not well? Or wait. Is she like me? Not very fond of meeting new people? Especially at a party? Hold on… Is it because of me? Shit! I might have stood on the sidewalk for too long. But…I didn't do it on purpose. It just happened, and I wasn't supposed to get caught. But she wouldn't realize that, would she? Maybe she thinks there are some creeps downstairs, so she doesn't want to make an appearance? What have I done? I shouldn't have said anything and let Mrs. Caul blow the candles. My mind rambled on without any brakes.

I heard the wooden staircase squeak, accompanied by Lalita's muffled voice. I began to tense up. What should I say to her if I get a chance to talk to her? The entire time I was there at the party, I looked forward to seeing her. I usually wanted to leave a party or any social gathering very early, but it was a little different that night. It could have been the first time I was so eager to meet someone in a long time. And the fact that she was a stranger to me came as a surprise even for myself. I couldn't get the image out of my mind—her beautiful figure as she stood near the window, the pretty features that I could delineate from a distance, the air of mystery about her as she looked straight at me through the open window. I tried to imagine her voice in my head. But I couldn't. I had to hear it for myself.

"Hey!" She greeted everyone as she walked towards the table. She had a soft, mellow voice.

"How are you, Maya? I can't believe you are home. Ha-ha." Kev said as he rushed towards her and Lalita.

"Ha-ha, I'm good. I'll be here for a while now, Kev." She said with a half-smile on her face. "How about you? I heard you graduated today," she said.

"Yup! Finally!" He laughed. They seemed to be pretty comfortable around each other. But I noticed a difference between how Kev acted around Lalita and Maya. He seemed a little more cautious with her.

"Hey, by the way, Maya, meet my buddy Gaurav. We graduated together today."

My mind had been partially dead when I saw her and heard her speak for the first time. Kev's comment shook me back to the room where we all stood.

"Hel..." I stuttered, struggling to speak any further. I cleared my throat and tried again, "Hello there!" I managed to get some words out of my mouth. Without my senses being aware, I had stretched out my right hand to her side for a handshake. I froze when I realized I had done that.

"Hey, Gaurav, nice to meet you!" She said, smiling. Then, she came a little closer to me and received my hands. It felt as though I had been struck by lightning. I saw nothing but her for those few moments. Her hands were warmer than mine, and I felt comforted by it. She let go of my hands and proceeded to talk to Lalita and Kev.

My inordinately apprehensive mind could not stop pondering about her perception of me. My instincts said that she recognized me as nothing but a mere stalker, a creep who is fascinated by her physical beauty. Deep down, I wished I could tell her how pleased I was to meet her finally, but my mind seemed to have been too occupied absorbing the sight of her breathtaking beauty.

Maya was a hurricane in the parrot-colored top and black pajama pants with polka dots. Her long, straight, midnight-black tresses gently flowed over her shoulders, draping her tapered waist like a soft blanket. A cute, dainty nose stretched gracefully between velvety soft cheeks, and a striking V-shaped chin sat proudly over the popping collar bones that peeped through her top. Her slender lips with a subtle touch of lip gloss on them jolted me every time they moved. Her smile was like a cool breeze on a hot summer day and an oasis for my soul, a shrine where I can purge my soul.

I studied her closely from where I stood. I stole glances at her, careful not to look too obvious. When she spoke, her mellifluous voice seemed like an innocent yet sinful melody—a perfect amalgamation of rhythm and harmony. It was like a spell that made me fixate on her very being. I tried to look away but to no avail. I knew I was a captive of her charm, a forlorn lover who has submitted to fate. As she leaned slightly forward towards the cake to take out the candles, I caught a delicate whiff of the zesty fragrance of her body which arrested my attention, slowing down my heartbeat to a kind of rhythm I wish I could retain forever. Her pretty eyes were like shining emeralds that could change any man's fate. As I looked into them, I felt myself falling down a deep hollow abyss, not the one that I dreaded but one that is hypnotic—an arcadia every man desires. Good Lord! How can someone look so devastatingly gorgeous from that up close? I thought to myself. Like an ardent devotee, I stood there and watched my muse of eternal poetry.

"Hey. Would you blow the candle out?" Someone said, patting my shoulder.

"Hmm?" I said abruptly and then heard myself asking, "What?"

"Our cake, mate! Blow the candle." Kev said.

"Oh! Yes, let's do it."

Hypnotized by the immense aura Maya's single glimpse carried, I never realized when Mrs. Caul cut the cake. She must have blown the candles out, and people must have clapped and sung. Some might have taken photographs with her, and a lot more must have happened without me being aware of any of it. It was my turn now, and as I blew the candle, everybody congratulated me for the umpteenth time. Those greetings and toasts seemed trivial compared to the extreme pleasure I derived from the very first sight of Maya. As I was leaving Mr. Caul's place, I glanced at Maya for the last time, who was still standing with the guests. From a distance, she looked like a miracle healer who could reinvigorate a marred soul.

My ears only received portions of her conversations with the people around her. She was explaining something about her visit to some city with her friends. "It was a pretty cool experience..." she said with a killer smile, and I couldn't catch the rest of her sentences after that. Mrs. Caul, on the other hand, was explaining to a family friend about Maya's habit of staying away from meetings such as this.

"You see... My Maya isn't particularly into all these parties I host occasionally," she laughed between her speech. "She prefers to be out and about somewhere else, doing something she likes. She doesn't like to stay long at home too. She's rather eager to see new things," she said.

I was awestruck by her! *Doesn't she like crowds? Are you saying we have something in common? Can she get any better than this? I need to know more about her!* My thoughts went wild.

I usually had a racy heart when I was among a crowd. The unknown faces of strangers had a way of distorting my mental wirings, rendering me helpless like a child. I had always known that about me. And I disliked how little I felt in a room full of people. But that night, my heart seemed to run a mile faster than it normally used to; but for reasons other than the crowd around me. I couldn't keep still. My legs grew restless each minute I glanced at her. I let out heavy sighs when nobody noticed me. Was this what I was waiting for? The fantasy from my younger days about the person I would fall in love with seemed to be standing at the doors of my empty heart.

She sat opposite to where I sat. Maybe it was just my faulty interpretation of her, but she seemed to feel uneasy somehow. Why wasn't she chattering away like the rest of the people around me? Why did she have that subtle smile on her lips—a smile I could not decipher, almost as if she had a million things running around her head that she wanted to keep only to herself. Could I ever be in a fraction of her myriad thoughts? I wondered.

I felt an urge surmounting under my chest to stand up and walk towards her and steal her away from the crowd just to talk for a moment or two, hear her sweet mellow voice again saying my name. She looked at me for a second, accidentally, of course. I froze. But I managed a smile—a sign of my soul reaching out to touch hers. She smiled back at me. It was the prettiest thing I had ever seen in my entire life. Why was it that when I stole glances at her, the world around me faded into a murmur, and only her face shone like a single colorful stroke of paint on a dark canvas?

The clock hands moved quicker than it usually did that night. The celebration ended, and we had to say our goodnights and goodbyes.

"Oww, thank you, everyone, for coming. I had a wonderful time!" Mrs. Caul said. Everyone started to bid farewell while I stood stiff as a stone beside Kev, who was still chattering away with Lalita. Maya stood behind her mom, looking absolutely stunning.

"Thanks, everyone!" She said brightly.

No, thank you, Maya. For gracing the party with your presence. You are so beautiful! Can I see you again? The words drowned between my lips, and all I could manage to say was a simple "Goodnight" while looking at her. She saw me too and said, "Good night, Gaurav. See you around."

I felt as though I had won the world. There was nothing else I needed that moment than her single 'Good night.' I was content.

On my way back home that night, I kept revisiting the craziness of the day's events—the ceremony, the sudden invitation to a party by Mrs. Caul, the hectic process of getting changed within an hour and catching the bus with Kev, but most of all, the dreamy woman I encountered. Maya. The very thought of her sent shivers down my spine, making my body tremble even in the heat of a summer night.

Kev voiced out in concern, "That soda must have given you a cold, buddy."

I looked at him and nodded in agreement. I knew those weren't shivers of cold but frissons of joy—the ones I got every time I thought about Maya.

"Nothing to worry about, Kev," I patted his back. After all, it was he who dragged me to the party. He was the unsung hero.

Knowing well that I would have a wonderful dream that would mark the happy ending of my graduation day, I went to bed that night, artlessly smiling.

That fateful night was the first time in my life that I felt that a party didn't have to come to an end.

~~*~~

The ocean of love, though vast and magnanimous in its beauty, is a treacherous place. It is riddled with strong currents pulling you towards them as you helplessly give in to their force. Drowning under them was my destiny, but floating around to admire the mesmerizing beauty of the corals underwater was my choice, for those depths felt like home—the depths of unrequited love.

Home is Where the Heart is!

To get a permanent residency in Canada, I had to work in a job for a year. I was having no luck in Vancouver, and it was only after I opened myself up for relocation that I got a job, which unfortunately was in a city three hours away. To travel between Vancouver and my new job, I had to cross a brief stretch of international waters, making the two seem much farther than they already were. I was so upset about not being able to find a job, but now that I had one, the feeling had only become worse. An inexplicable, unsettling dread set in. Vancouver was only three hours away, and it's not like I had any close family or friends other than Kev there. Well, of course, there was also Mrs. Caul and Lalita and…

My thoughts were interrupted by my ringing cell phone.

"Hi Maa, how are you?"

"Gaurav beta, your useless brother forgot to pay the power bill on time again. So, I thought I'd talk to the son who turned out okay," she laughed as I heard Aman groan in the background. "You tell me, beta, how are you?"

"I got a job in Victoria," my voice dropped at the last part of the sentence.

"That's great! I'm so proud of you!" Her voice went a pitch higher.

"Well, I'm not exactly working at an IT company Maa. It's only a small job at Burger King."

"So what? It's only the beginning. Every job has value and should be treated as such. Besides, once you get your residency, I'm sure you'll get the job you want in no time, with your diploma."

"Yeah," I said absentmindedly.

"Are you okay, beta? You seem distracted."

"Yeah, no… I mean, I'm busy thinking about moving and everything. I'll talk to you later, okay? Love you." I hung up. I felt guilty for doing that, but my mind was too restless to pretend everything was okay.

Maya and I hadn't spoken or met since those few awkward seconds at the party, but now and then, she would play at the back of my mind like a nostalgic melody I cherished well. The migration between the two cities seemed more brutal than my relocation to a different country. I knew shifting to Victoria would mean having zero chances of meeting her again for several months. It was a price I was not ready to pay.

Do I have to be stuck on that island for a year? Why can't I just do any job and become eligible for residency? I paid a fortune to get a diploma; just grant me permanent residence already. Damn these immigration policies! How far exactly is that city from Vancouver? Google Maps says three hours. What if there's an emergency? Will I be able to come back on short notice if anyone needs me here? Who exactly would need me here? I guess me being or not being here doesn't really make a difference to anyone.

I had never felt so helplessly annoyed. There was nothing that could change the reality. I knew I had to go to Victoria the following day. The more I thought about leaving Vancouver, the more I felt my spirit dwindling in the agony of parting from my chances of meeting Maya again.

I don't even know her! But why do I feel so dejected? This is stupid, Gaurav! I tortured and reasoned inside my mind… It felt like a separation from something crucial in my life. It felt close to that feeling when I first left Delhi behind—an emptiness like a waterless pond or a leafless tree. I went to sleep with the memory of her voice still resounding like a siren in my mind.

The next morning, I left for Victoria with the determination that I would keep her in my thoughts every day and that the distance between us is but a mere illusion.

~~*~~

Settling in the new town wasn't that tough, unlike when I came to Vancouver. Although, coming to peaceful terms with the infinite stirring thoughts in my mind had become a daily challenge. I'd often think about Vancouver, which almost always led me to think about Maya. There was so little I knew about her, yet she somehow managed to occupy a large part of my day. I recalled how she sat at her desk, fixated on her laptop. Was she working? What was she studying? Every day I thought of her and fabricated tiny details about her like how she took her morning coffee with almond milk and sugar or how she hated ketchup but could not have her fries without them, or how she tucked her hair behind her ear when she was nervous or uncomfortable. I wondered if I would ever find out if any of these were true.

Was she still home? I wondered. Maybe she left to find a job too? Maybe I should just see her once to clear my conscience, I thought.

Meanwhile, the job wasn't going great either. Working at Burger King isn't the best idea for a vegetarian. Watching hundreds of people devour their whoppers was already quite taxing but having to watch them cook the meat every single day was becoming unbearable.

Hoping every day that I would soon be back in Vancouver, I never gave up on my search for a job. Five painful months crawled by before I finally got one. However, I knew that Kev had found a new roommate by then. He had hoped that I stayed in Vancouver, but I had no choice but to leave. And so, he had to find someone to share the rent with instead of me. It bummed me terribly, but I had no right to ask for his company again. He had his worries in life too. Those years with him in the rental had been precious. I realized how I had taken his presence for granted. Kev was a good friend to me, and I realized it so much more when I moved away from Vancouver.

And so, despite not having found a place to stay yet, I decided to go back.

I felt dreadful at the thought of hunting for a place to stay, yet again. A week before I left for Vancouver, I felt the sudden urge to ring up Mrs. Caul. She had always been resourceful at times like these. Surely, she would know someone who might have a basement to rent. I was hopeful but sorry at the same time. I hadn't been in touch with her for a while, and so I felt terribly guilty that I was calling her only when I found myself in a tight situation.

Oh, how she must think of me. I must be a nuisance to her! I thought as the call rang from the other end of the line. It sounded like a fire alarm echoing in my ear caves for some reason.

"Hello! Mrs. Caul! How are you?" I tried to sound as confident as possible.

"Hey! I am good, Gaurav. How have you been? I haven't heard from you in ages!"

The guilt crept up again behind my back.

"I've been okay, Auntie. I'm sorry for not telling you sooner…" I briefed her about my move to Victoria and Kev's new roommate and my return to Vancouver in the coming week.

"That's great news, Gaurav! Do you want me to come to pick you up from the ferry terminal?"

"No, no, that's okay. Right now, I need somewhere to go from the ferry terminal."

"What do you mean?"

"I don't have a place in Vancouver yet. But I'm looking for it." You're supposed to ask her for her help right away, you fool!

"Oh, that!" She paused for two seconds.

"Don't worry about it. You can stay in our house."

"Thank you so much for the offer, Mrs. Caul, but I'll have to look for a long-term rental anyway. Might as well do it now, so I don't have to move twice."

"No, silly, that's not what I meant. You can stay at our house. You're absolutely welcome," she said.

My mouth gaped in disbelief. I couldn't respond right away.

"Are you serious?"

"Ha-ha. Of course. Unless you don't want to," she said, almost like a tease.

"Of course not!" I responded. "I just...didn't think...this could happen..." I mumbled. She laughed again.

"If Kev can stay with us, definitely you can too. Until you make further plans for your career."

"That's so...Wow. Thank you." That was all the words I could manage, reeling from the utter shock.

After some more conversation over the phone, she bade goodnight to me.

"Goodnight, Mrs. Caul. I'll call you when I am on the ferry. Bye."

What! What just happened? Did she really mean I could stay with them, in their house, for the long term? Should I call her again to confirm? How did she make such an important decision so quickly? She must be joking. But why would she do that? Didn't she need to discuss it with everyone else? I should still keep looking for a rental, just in case she changes her mind. I will keep looking for a place. This can't be real!

I immediately checked my phone to make sure I had dialed the correct number. Her offer made me feel relieved and uneasy at the same time. But how could I possibly refuse such a ginormous offer? It was all too good to be true, and it made me fearful, as though my house of cards were ready to be tumbled down.

The next few days were spent packing and planning. Even though I had decided to keep looking for rentals, I couldn't muster the time and energy to do so. I was so occupied and excited by the idea of living in Vancouver again that I never even realized how the days turned into nights. Suddenly, it dawned upon me that I would be living under the same roof as Maya. I felt a slight tingle of joy as she lingered in the realms of my mind, driving me to a state of blissful stupor. Strange energy enlivened my soul again and, in a minute, I found myself engrossed in envisaging a life with the woman I admire. I had no power over the reveries her name produced in my head.

I jumped out of joy, and a second later, fear barged in. The fear of being too close to the light, of being startled by the enormity of her energy. A hundred different scenarios of our second meeting overwhelmed my mind with every breath. I imagined and reimagined a hundred different conversations with her with every heartbeat.

The week that seemed like the longest seven days of my life finally ended, and I found myself on the ferry to Vancouver.

As I came out of the terminal, I spotted Mrs. Caul waving at me. She wore a long black coat to compensate for the windy November weather. Her shades were perfectly made to tackle some sunshine —not too black, yet dark enough. As a go-getter and someone with a nerve of steel, Mrs. Caul took on life as a master. "Thank you for coming."

"Oh, no worries. I don't have much work these days. How was the ferry ride? Enjoyed the view?"

I didn't even realize when Vancouver arrived. I was so lost, wondering what the situation at your home would be like.

"Yes. Breathtaking scenery all the way." I lied.

"We had a relative from India visiting us this past week, so we weren't able to set up your room. Would you mind staying in the guest room for a couple of days until we can fix up your room?"

"Yes. Of course!"

Have you told Lalita & Maya about my arrival? You must have told them. What was their reaction? What did they say to you? Were they okay with it? Please tell me something about it. Okay, just tell me how Maya reacted. She must have said something, anything?

My thoughts roared like a waterfall as we sat in her car and breezed past the familiar landscapes of Vancouver.

"I made rice and dal for you, Gaurav," she said in the car. Her sweetness reminded me once again of my mother back home.

"Oh! I would like that so much. I have been eating frozen food and Maggi for so many months now."

"Bwa...ha...ha...ha!" She laughed, well aware of my cooking abilities. "I'm going to have to force you into the kitchen with me. You cannot be an adult if you have to rely on me for a proper meal."

She gave me a good tour of the commute, swiftly dodging the endlessly zipping city traffic with her SUV. Though Victoria was calmer and more scenically beautiful, Vancouver felt like home. We arrived at her place sooner than expected. I felt carsick suddenly; at least that's what I hoped it was. Several unexplainable sensations rose and faded inside me. I could feel the blood rushing to my ears, heightening my emotions, pushing them all the way to the top of the Himalayas and then bringing them all the way down into the deep trenches of the oceans the very next second. My body felt the cold of the Arctic immediately after it experienced the scorching heat of the Sahara sun. We passed the cemetery, leaving its lush green grass behind quicker than the last time I had seen it, making me want to jump out of the car.

Mrs. Caul's house was modern and well-furnished with laminate wood flooring and classic furniture. There was a strange Indianness about that house. One could almost feel that Mrs. Caul had carried the essence of her native country, across the oceans, to a foreign land. A touch of the West merged with the native spirit of the East to create an alluring haven of tranquility. Mrs. Caul, a retired woman in her late 50's, was someone with extreme enthusiasm. While the daughters kept themselves busy for a few weeks at work and school before the Christmas holidays, she kept herself engaged by attending weddings and participating in charity work. Visiting the Gurudwara every Sunday morning was her ritual. Unlike me, Mrs. Caul was gregarious and could easily engage in friendly banter with anyone she met.

I followed Mrs. Caul as she walked to the back door, closing the garage after parking the car. Each stride consumed more energy than the previous, each step heavier than the last. As she inserted the key into the hole, I braced myself for the impact. In a minute, I was engrossed in deep thought, pondering about how I could strike up a conversation.

'Hey, how is it going?'
Nope! Too generic.
'Hello!'
'Hello there!'
'Hi! How are you?' Na, too cold.
'How have you been?'

Is this how I am going to meet and greet her? Like I am meeting some unimportant colleague? What is she supposed to even reply to that? 'I am fine,' 'I am good,' or just 'Hello!'? And then be about her business. This isn't how I want it to be. Oh! Shit, the door has opened.

Fuck!

Breathe, breathe…

"Nobody's home." Mrs. Caul's voice rang in my ears, creating a paradox of joy and disappointment.

"Oh, okay," I said, trying to sound as relaxed as possible.

"Lalita's at work, and Maya has classes."

"Oh!" I let out a sigh of relief, gradually feeling the toffee-brown floor under my feet.

I had been in that house before, so I was familiar with the ground floor layout. Curious to know where my actual room would be, I asked Mrs. Caul if I could just take a look at my room. Maybe I would be fine with whatever condition it was in. She showed me the upstairs. I peeked in my room which was in the middle of two bigger rooms, and it wasn't what I expected it to be.

Many books and crayons were scattered on an old wooden table. A few plastic bags filled with waste paper and stationery watched me silently from the corner, patiently waiting for a gust of wind to ruffle them. A big, round mirror atop the table invited me to look at it so that it could tell the onlooker that it needed cleaning. As I flicked the light switch on, two out of the four bulbs didn't show any sign of life. The remaining faintly glowed as if planning to give up on me soon. The carpet had to be vacuumed—a little bit of cleaning and arranging had to be done. The bed frame laden with a sunken mattress longed for a plush one. A dull bedsheet tried hard to cover for the embarrassment it endured.

"Let me help you set up this room, Auntie. And in the meantime, I can stay downstairs until it gets done."

"Okay." She said and continued, "So the room to your right is kind of an office space with a TV. The one on your left is where Maya stays…"

Woah… this is her room? And this is mine, right next to hers? NO! I am not ready for this. My heart is going to explode…

…Across the staircase is the master bedroom…" She continued, oblivious to my panic.

"Umm…" I regained my mental composure. "…this won't need much work. I can just arrange and clean it today."

"What's the rush, dear? I wanted to replace the mattress and do a little bit of carpet cleaning," she said.

"I can just vacuum it for now. The mattress looks fine." I said, sitting on the edge of the bed, "See? It is fine."

"Okay. Whatever you want." The wooden staircase made a squeaking noise as she stepped on them, "Come down for lunch, or I'll have to heat everything again."

"Yes, yes. Coming!"

As I was descending the stairs, a sweet aroma of freshly cooked rice and dal complemented with salad and pickles enveloped the dining room, invigorating every bit of my soul. I helped myself with a spoonful of every delicacy, and in a minute, my plate full of food appeared beautiful with a blend of different shades. Each bite subtly dissolved in my mouth and took me to a state of trance. Mrs. Caul's hands were pure magic. Her kitchen was a wonderland.

~~*~~

After enjoying a hearty meal, I decided to clean my room. I rushed upstairs without wasting another minute, but the unkempt condition of the room drained my soul. I stood there staring blankly at the dreary and dusty room—a discolored, time-worn space that has endured hurricanes or perhaps sheltered the tantrums of a young child. Shrugging the thoughts away, I slowly started by cleaning up the table. I picked up the books and placed them carefully in a box one by one. A mason jar sheltered the broken crayons scattered all over the table, painting it in an array of colors. New ones replaced the broken bulbs and the antique mirror longing for a wipe sparkled when cleaned with a silk cloth. I smiled in its reflection as the tomb-like cold room started to breathe again, promising me the rest and warmth I needed. An hour waltzed by as I stared at the ceiling, thinking about how my plans had drastically changed overnight.

I rushed to take a peek downstairs whenever I heard the front door open, making sure I didn't miss Maya when she came, but she didn't. Finally, after doing so around seventeen times in a couple of hours, I gave up. I didn't want it to seem too obvious that I was eagerly waiting for them at the door like a puppy awaiting his master's return. Lalita arrived first, and I went down to meet her.

"Ha-ha. Welcome, welcome, Gaurav! Good to have you here," she greeted me like an old buddy, calming my agitated nerves. We exchanged a few words. She seemed tired and went straight to her room to rest. I expected her to say something more about my move to their house, but she didn't say anything. It seemed very normal for her to see me at the house. I didn't know what to expect as a reaction from them, making me more agitated. I then looked at my phone and saw how late it was. I went back to my room and tried to relax, but my heart would not allow it until I saw her face to face.

She's been gone for more than ten hours now. What university teaches for so long on Fridays? Even the teachers are probably home by now. Should I ask Mrs. Caul if it's normal for her to be this late? No, I should probably wait for another half an hour. Nobody seems to be worried about her here. My head swirled with worry and doubt.

Lalita was listening to some weird music in her room, and Mrs. Caul was downstairs on the couch, switching between watching TV and staring at her phone.

Could she be hanging out with her friends? Why not? It's a Friday. Could she be stuck in traffic—maybe? Has she met with an accident… no, no, no! She has been driving for so long. But what if an idiot caused it, and she's affected? Fuck! I wouldn't know where she is right now because I don't even have her number. Man! I just hope she is okay. She should at least call her mom…Oh Gaurav, just relax! Even her family knows she'll be alright.

Then suddenly, I heard the stairway creek. Someone was coming up. My reflexes went berserk, and I stood up in a flash and went to the door like a kid hoping to see Santa with his long-awaited gifts.

"Hey!" Maya said the moment I opened my door. She was standing just a few steps away from my door.

"Hello… Maya!" I replied instinctively, startled by her voice. Only she and God would know the type of expression I had on my face when I saw her. There was an awkward silence between us for an indefinite amount of time.

"Good to see you again." Both of us said together. It felt straight out of a movie when I realized what had happened.

She chuckled softly. "Mom said you'll be here for a while. Welcome, Gaurav!" The words from her mouth came to me like the melody of a song.

"Thank you. Uh…I hope it's not too much of a bother for you all," I said in a soft tone. My throat felt dry suddenly. Why was I speaking so softly? I didn't understand.

"Oh, not at all." She said with a subtle smile as she casually turned around and went to her door.

A familiar fragrance brushed against me, heartily welcoming me to a new beginning.

I went back inside my room and recalled our quick interaction, her voice repeatedly playing in my mind. It struck the innermost chord of my soul every time it fell on my ears. She was there! Right next to my room! The walls were thick, so it was pretty soundproof, but when I shut my eyes and listened carefully, I could hear some shuffling sounds of her movements in the room. I felt painfully separated from her because of the wall between us. Still, at the same time, I was thankful that I was far enough from her to be safe from being perpetually intoxicated and paralyzed in her presence.

After a short nap, I stepped out of my room and found her standing near the staircase, fidgeting with her phone. The loud thud of the door startled her, and she looked back at me and said, "Oh! Hi."

"Hi. Going somewhere?" I was elated on seeing her.

"Yeah. Are you hungry? Want me to get you anything from McDonald's?"

It took me a second to reply. They didn't have any vegetarian items that suited my palate as far as I know.

"Oh, no. I'm okay." I smiled at her.

"How about ice cream?" She said as she slowly made her way down the stairs.

"Wait, ice cream?" I said before she left my sight.

"Yeah," she said, turning to me again.

"Can I come with you?" I said, completely baffled at myself for asking her such a question. My body and mind seemed to work separately when I saw her. I regretted it instantly.

Oh no, Gaurav. You fool! What if she wants to go alone? You just met her for the 2nd time! Why do you have to be so bold all of a sudden?

"Sure! Let's go," she said.

I jumped out of my skin upon getting her permission. I didn't care about the ice cream. It was the anticipation of being with her in her car that arrested my bones. It wasn't just butterflies in my stomach. There was an entire zoo in there as I walked down to the door with her. Car rides had always been refreshing—but one with her would take hold of my senses entirely.

Her car was more than a metal chassis on four wheels—it was a living object, experiencing its reality. Its vanilla-white paint resembled her snow-white skin; the rounded LED headlamps sparkled as though imitating her eyes, and the aerodynamic curves on its reinforced body reminded me of her waist. It had its own personality, like it was meant to be Maya's car—not a dot more, not a dot less. She stepped in it like a rockstar entering an arena. When it moved, a rush of air carried a sweet fragrance to my lungs, like the dispersed air carried whenever Maya glided by.

"So, Mom said you got a job here?" She said, starting the engine, looking fine as hell.

"Yeah, it's going to help in immigration."

"That's good. Good luck!"

"Thank you," I said. I was going through a hurricane of thoughts. I had prepared a conversation in my head, but nothing seemed to last in her presence. I couldn't organize them in order. She wasn't much of a talker, which made me feel pressured to initiate. Then suddenly, she stunned me with the most unexpected question—

"Are you single?" She said, looking straight ahead, unfazed by the words she had uttered.

"Ha?" I pretended as though I didn't catch her question well. I was too shocked for words.

"Are you single?" She repeated coolly.

"Yes…I am?" I replied.

"I see," she said. I didn't know how to read her. What did she mean by her simple "I see"? Why did she ask me that question out of the blue? Was it just me? Or am I just so divorced from the normality of casual conversations that I find the smallest of things weird and awkward? I had no means of knowing.

And you Maya? Are you single? Tell me you are, even though it is hard to believe. How can you not be adored and loved, let alone not liked? Is it a guy from your class? Or perhaps someone you met online? Someone must have asked you out for sure. There are so many brave guys out there, unlike me, whose greatest struggle right now is asking you if you are single, even though you asked first.

I wasn't sure why I couldn't bring myself to ask her. Perhaps I was too nervous or perhaps fearful that she might have someone. In that case, I'd rather be clueless.

The car brisked through the empty driveway and stopped at the ordering machine.

"One vanilla sundae and small fries, please." She turned to face me. "What do you want?

"Whatever you are having. Not the fries, though."

"Sorry, make it two sundaes and small fries. On Mastercard, thank you!"

We waited for our order. She drew her hair back in a sassy manner and leaned back on the leather of her seat. She slowly began to tap her fingers on the steering wheel. I could see that she was slightly anxious.

"Icecream is such a great stress buster." She blurted out.

"Agreed," I said, not wasting any second.

"Why? What happened? Are you stressed?" I asked.

"I am going for an internship in a remote town. It is a requisite in finishing my degree."

"Remote town?" I asked, a little confused.

"Yeah. It's quite far off, but an excellent opportunity for me to build my career."

"Hmm...I see. That sounds cool!" I tried to sound as normal as I could be.

"Yeah. But I haven't told mom yet. She worries too much."

I did not know how to respond to this news. I could feel a burn in my chest.

"When are you going, Maya?"

"In a month or two. Hehe," she replied.

Two months! It took me some time to maintain my composure so that she does not see the despair I was feeling.

"For how long?"

"Five months."

"Oh...Okay."

My heart sank completely. We had our ice-creams inside the car. I felt my body cooling down rapidly.

"You were right. It does help." I said, finally breaking the silence. I had finished almost half of the ice cream.

"What?" She looked at me.

"Icecream does help to bust the stress," I said, looking down.

"I know, right!" She said, letting out a cute laugh from her pretty lips, which ringed in my ears for a few seconds.

The ride back home was near-silent, partially because she munched on the fries. The cumbersome weight resting on my chest got heavier with each turn the car took. Despite her being right next to me, all I could think of was her being gone. The thought grew heavier with every passing minute, and I could feel everything around me becoming a blur, distorting my vision of the coming few months. I looked straight at the bustling road, and the only thing my eyes perceived was the blues. The ticking of my watch kept reminding me of the cruel fact, and I found myself lost in its tempo, imagining a dystopic world that had atrociously separated me from my precious lover. I knew I had to cherish the present moment with her in the car. But the thought of her absence became the bigger tyrant in my head.
We entered the house and found Mrs. Caul and Lalita watching television together.

"Ha-ha! So, the two quiet ones went out for a stroll, huh?" Lalita giggled. I felt my blood rising to my cheeks.

"Yeah, we went to get ice cream," she said coolly, walking past them and into the kitchen.

"Let's make dinner, shall we?" Mrs. Caul said as she comfortably stretched from the couch.

My first evening with them felt like a dream. It felt too good to be true.

Over dinner that night, they talked about Maya and her plans. Lalita and Mrs. Caul wanted Maya to stay and find something in or near the city.

"I haven't thought about it yet, guys. I'll find one soon," she said, slowly munching on her salad, looking down. I could see her looking a little worried. Half of me wanted her to listen to them and stay in Vancouver, but the other half rooted for her to go anywhere she wanted as long as she would be happy.

Shortly after dinner, we went to our rooms.

"Goodnight," she said as she went towards her door.

"You too, Maya," I said, and before she left my sight, I gathered all the guts I had in the world to say a few words to her.

"Oh, and hey…" I said, trying to sound as friendly as possible.

"Hope you're not too stressed about it. Your internship, I mean. Don't worry. It'll be fine." I said it in such a robotic manner that I wanted to drown myself in an ocean of lava. Why am I like this?

"Oh…" she said, looking a little surprised.

"Thanks for that, Gaurav," she replied with the warmest smile I have ever laid eyes upon. I stood there in a trance even after she shut her door.

I laid in bed that night mostly awake, pondering about the girl next door—her exquisite beauty, her laugh, her calm demeanor, her smile that made me go crazy. As the hands of the clock went past midnight, my eyelids weighed ten times more upon me than they did during the day and gravity dragged me to the borderlands of the world of dreams, but I fought it. I wouldn't let sleep flex its wings until the light in her room turned off.

~~*~~

I was woken up by a series of "fee-bee" sounds. As I opened my eyes, I saw a black bird perched on a branch of the maple tree. Having no idea what time of day it was and for how long I had slept, I got up frantically thinking how I was definitely going to be late on my first day at work. Then I realized that it was Saturday today and   I wasn't starting until Monday. What a relief. It would have left a bad impression if I had turned up late. I couldn't help glancing at the bird once again, which sang happily. This bird didn't have to worry about being late to work, making a career, or managing its finances. It was free to do what it pleased.

I am going to make the most of this weekend, like this bird.

I got out the bed with this thought in mind. Unfortunately, no matter how lightly I put my feet on the wooden staircase to not wake everyone up on a weekend morning, it creaked loudly. Embarrassed and ashamed as I took each step, I regretted jinxing my enthusiasm for making the most of that day. Downstairs in the hall, Maya was tying her shoe laces downstairs in the hall.

"Hey!" I exclaimed.

"Good morning!" she replied.

"Are you going for a run?" I casually asked.

"I was thinking of going for a walk. Would you like to come?" she asked.

Today is starting out well for me, I thought. It was hard not to nod vigorously in agreement several times when I imagined myself spending time with her.

Once we had walked around for a few minutes, I realized how unprepared I was for the icy breeze. Still, the joy of being right next to Maya was enough to keep me going. . Contrary to my assumptions, Central Park was already crowded with morning walkers, joggers, and children playing loudly. Although I was so overwhelmed by the crowd and wanted to leave immediately, I secretly wished for our walk to last longer than usual. My feet never touched the ground when I accompanied her, as if I were soaring high with each step. I enjoyed hearing about the different parts of the park from her. My stamina wasn't as great as Maya's though and every time we passed by empty benches in the park, my feet tingled and I longed to take a little break. Unconsciously, I might have stared at one of the unoccupied benches for too long during our second round as she shook her head and said, "I hope you're not tired."

"Oh, not at all. This park is a lot bigger than I expected. But I'm fine." I lied straight through my teeth.

"I come for a walk here sometimes."

Walking was one of the least interesting things in the world to me. I would rather run or sit at home. There was no in between. *If I am stepping out of the house, I would rather do some cardio. How can someone go for just a walk?* I wondered.

"Is that so? I would like to accompany you if you don't mind. I enjoy walking, it's healthy, and I rarely do it, so..." Only I knew how hesitantly I replied.

"Haha, why would I mind? Not sure what our schedule would look like though." She pondered, and then an awkward silence followed for a few seconds. She smiled and nodded softly while staring at my face, saying, "But I'll wait for you to come back from work."

"Oh! Perfect." I grinned with excitement as we strolled on our way back home. This way I could spend more time with her.

As we continued our walk, I couldn't help but feel that I wanted to ask her about something that piqued my curiosity yesterday. Ever since then my chest had been feeling heavy yet I couldn't summon the courage to ask her directly. As the distance to home decreased, I felt increasingly uneasy. I couldn't hold it in anymore once I saw the house approaching quickly.

"Hey, Maya." I exclaimed.

"Yeah?"

"Are you single?" I felt the ground beneath me split apart. I couldn't even move my neck out of embarrassment to look at her as she laughed generously at my question.

"I am now." She replied as she raised her brows at me, , "Why didn't you ask that yesterday?"

I scratched my head and mumbled, "I guess I was distracted by the ice cream."

"Hmm... great priorities in life, Gaurav!" she teased me as she laughed out loud. Then she brought her iPhone out of her pocket and clicked a quick selfie of us. I was clueless as to why she would do that. I wasn't even looking at the camera but the sidewalk, like a robot. "I like this athleisure outfit on you." She said as pointed her finger at my clothing. "Thanks!" I said smiling ear to ear. A part of me was still bustling with curiosity to know what had exactly transpired between her and her ex but that didn't even matter as the joy of knowing she was single provided me enough relief for the day.

Come rain or shine, heading out for a walk together had become our ritual after that. Maya would wait for me on days when I got home late from work. We mostly chatted and laughed on our walks, but we also complained about first world problems such as not getting enough rebates on electric cars during some of them. As opposed to what I had assumed, the sensation I felt while in her vicinity did not fade with time. It took different feels and moods but it was there all the time. After a few weeks, I realized walking in that crowded park wasn't all that bad, it was certainly better than staying at home and regretting not going with Maya. After a while, I even started looking forward to walking with her whenever she planned to go for it, knowing that it wouldn't last long once she moved to the remote town.

~~*~~

As days went by, I gradually loosened up to the absurd reality of living under the same roof as Maya. But that didn't mean that I could approach her casually. No matter how much I tried, I turned into an awkward alien every time I saw her pass by.

One evening, I sat with Mrs. Caul on the couch and talked about some random stuff that happened that day. I realized more things about her living under her roof. I learned how Mrs. Caul loved sitting on the same couch every night, religiously browsing through Facebook. She was more active on social media than any of us in the house. Not a day would go by without her checking out her accounts, wishing birthdays, posting as per the occasion, and engaging with friends online. She came from the conservative Indian society of the seventies, which was largely unwelcome to the things she was interested in. Luckily, the West gave her potential, the wings she needed to blossom. However, that didn't mean that her life was completely comfortable. I could see that she fought her own battles against family and outsiders alike even in the present. Being born in India in a generation that bridged the gap between the older and the younger generation, I realized that I could relate more with her on many topics that would otherwise be scorned upon back home.

I also saw how Lalita resembled Mrs. Caul to a large extent. They were both friendly and social, yet they had that resilience about them. I often thought about how she would think and look just like Lalita if Mrs. Caul were to be born again in the next life.

Maya, too had that quality of resilience and courage about her, like her mother and sister. But as time went by, I saw that she was more on the quiet and reserved side of things. She was jovial when she had to be, but she had those moments when she retreated to a world of her own, where no one seemed to reach her. Certainly not me. I was equally fascinated and fearful of her. I longed to get a glimpse of her innermost soul, but I didn't know how to navigate through my mental puzzle. I longed for her, but from a distance.

I fell in love with a few things I could relish from a distance, like the zesty nature of her natural scent every time she moved past the house and the way her eyes glimmered when she talked about something she liked to do. She put time and space to a halt whenever she moved her lips to say my name.

~~*~~

One Sunday, I went downstairs a little later than my usual routine. I had been on my phone for too long, and it was almost noon. I had gotten into the habit of waking up early. Not that I liked it, but work left no other choice. So, the idea of being even a minute late to something made me agitated, even on weekends.

I didn't mean to spend my only day off staying in my room like Lalita and Maya, who usually stepped out of their rooms only to eat. So, I went down quietly to see if everyone was there.

"Good afternoon, Beta." Mrs. Caul yelled from the couch. They all looked at me. I felt uneasy and nervous all of a sudden.

"Glad to see you're alive, Gaurav. Ha-ha." Lalita teased. Maya silently smiled at her comment. That undecipherable smile melted my soul each time I saw it.

"I had no idea it's already noon," I said as I awkwardly went to sit somewhere a little far from them.

The chair I was seated on was across the sofa and gave a panoramic view of everyone gathered—a rare event in the house. It was not a regular sight to see them gathered together cozily in one room.

Lalita sat plopped on the couch as she had just returned from her morning gym schedule. Beside her, Mrs. Caul sipped herbal tea. She had a long day at the gurudwara. Maya sat between them, going through a bunch of magazines like a posh fashion designer, momentarily checking her phone. I sipped on a glass of orange juice. My eyes darted to where she sat in the room. Each tiny muscle in her face worked together to maintain its enchantment. It was a look that was so stable yet capable enough to rattle my faculties at the very sight of it. That sweet face was such a small part of her, yet it carried a massive force of attraction. It was as though the sculptor took his time carving a masterpiece. Maya was a healer— for the self, me, and the world around her.

I felt a dull ache pulling on the muscles of my heart with the sudden realization that she would be leaving soon. Precious moments with her were slipping through my fingers.

~~*~~

I picked the stardust you left behind and made phantoms of you in my head. I ran after the echoes of your soul—too swift for my feeble legs to catch up to. Even my shadow yearns for your lips to say my name. You steady me like an anchor in the vastness of my dark waters, yet you crumble me like a delicate flower under a roaring cloudburst. I close my eyes and dance with the memory of you. And for that moment, I am home.

Farewell

"It's not that easy, Maya." Mrs. Caul said.

"One or two hours might be okay, but not eight, Maya," Lalita added in a demanding manner.

"Yeah! Eight is a lot. Even I wouldn't do it." Mrs. Caul said.

"But mom…I need it." Maya insisted.

"Get another one," Lalita suggested.

"What? While this one just sits right here?"

"There would be a lot of snow." Mrs. Caul said.

"It's not safe for you," Lalita said.

"I… don't know what to do," Maya said. She looked visibly troubled.

My heart ached at the slightest signs of distress on her face. I wanted to barge in and ask them what was wrong. But I had no right to do such a thing. I felt utterly helpless. Right then, Mrs. Caul saw me standing idly by the stairs.

"What do you think, Gaurav?" Mrs. Caul said, looking at me intently. All three of them stared at me in anticipation. I regretted standing there altogether.

"Sorry, I am not sure," I said, perplexed.

"Yeah, see! It's not an easy decision, Maya."

"No! I mean, I don't know what you are talking about."

"Maya wants to drive her car to where she is going in a few days. She needs a car there." Lalita said, uncovering the mystery of that day's big debate.

"Oh…" That was all I could manage.

Oh! First-world problems. I got worked up for no reason.

"Hey, Maya can fly there while her car could be transported in a truck, you know. Let me check how much it costs." I said, opening Safari on my phone.

"I suggested the same thing earlier," Lalita said.

"Umm…so, what's the problem?"

"She is having a hard time making up her mind," Mrs. Caul said, pointing at Maya. She looked away from our gaze with a tinge of red on her cheeks.

She's having a hard time deciding between flying and driving? How cute can you be, my sweet Maya?

I pretended not to notice her flushed cheeks.

"Here. This company can do it." I said, passing my phone to Maya.

"Oh…Can you send me the link?"

"Sure. What's your number?" I asked, clenching my jaw to brace for well-expected reactions from everyone. I don't remember if I'd ever asked a girl for her number like that. Nothing happened. Nobody said anything; nobody gave me weird stares, not even her. My pounding heart seemed to make my body tremble. But I continued to maintain my composure.

"Here, type in your number for me. I'll text you." She said, handing me her phone. I took it from her hands with a slight tremble. Our fingers brushed against each other, hers were colder than mine, and it sent shivers down my spine. I felt giddy.

604...499...1805. I typed in slowly, trying my best not to mess it up. I can't believe this is happening.

Gaurav, what have you been taking these days?

"Done!"

"Okay, thanks. I've texted you. Could you please forward me that link?" She asked.

I saw it. Two little letters that had enough power in them to move the tides of my heart.

"Sent!" I confirmed.

I didn't know what it was about Maya that made me cross the boundaries I had neatly kept for myself. With her, I became reckless. At least for me. Her name sat on my phone like a gemstone.

When I was a boy, grandma gifted me a blue car on my birthday. It was big enough for my tiny butt to fit in perfectly. I would sit on it for hours each day, roaring mad, mimicking the sounds that cars made. I would paddle it until my legs gave up. Whenever I went away from it to take a shower, eat, or sleep, I tied its wheel to the mango tree in our backyard with a rope that grandma gave me. Whenever it rained, I covered it with a plastic sheet without worrying about myself getting soaked. When it got dusty, I cleaned it with soap and water— giving it a proper bath. Sometimes, mom would playfully ask me if she could sit in my car. Each time she asked me, I would paddle it far away from her and stay aloof until she promised she wouldn't ask for it again. Nobody, not even grandma, could lay hands on my car, for I protected it with my life.

Maya's casual little 'hi' on my phone made me live that emotion all over again, for it gave me so much more than just a number. I felt I had to embrace it tightly under my arms before it was taken away from me. Her number was a passage connecting my world to hers. A key to tuning into her life; an escape route for when I couldn't control my firing mind; a path leading me to the abode of her heart. The purpose of having a phone got well-served that day because, in her text message, the kid in me found his most prized possession.

~~*~~

Even before I could open my eyes, I heard the tinkling of bells and ruffling, as if someone swept the floor with a giant broom. The city seemed like a perpetual expanse of the snowfield outside the window. Cars treading on the powdery snow made a muffled sound of damp crackers. Christmas had arrived. Mrs. Caul set up a tall IKEA tree in the living room that bloomed with colorful gifts and stockings. A miniature village flourished on the dining table. Its dwellers—men, women, animals, and spirits celebrated the birth of a miraculous baby. I opened the door to feel the warmth of the winter sun but had to shut it immediately as frosty wind clutched my senses, making me appreciate the coziness that the house nurtured.

A sweet and spicy smell swirled around the hall, leading me to the kitchen where Lalita brewed peppermint coffee. As I stepped out of the kitchen, Maya hastily walked past me. She stopped abruptly to look back, and in a minute, her lips curled into a gracious smile. Unlike that swag-bellied Santa, she looked gorgeous in her sweater with greens and reds in abundance and her fluffy leggings. She would probably nibble on some cookies, make her tea, and maybe help Lalita prepare for a special dinner. Knowing how to lift the season's spirits, Mrs. Caul set up a record that played Christmas music. The house glimmered with vintage lights and seasonal decor, swapping its modernity with centuries-old tradition for one day.

I couldn't tell myself if it was a feeling of loss or a loss of senses that had been stirring up my mind amidst the seasonal festivities. A sickness in my stomach came in waves rather than simply one stretch of pain. At first, it stayed there. Then it crouched up to the chest, and as days passed by, it pounced on my brain. It wasn't some medical issue that would go away once I saw a doctor. It was something underneath my conscious mind that needed healing. It never allowed me to sit still in tranquility.

Fear gripped me as I began to contemplate a life without Maya. In the vast emptiness of the world, I found myself lonely and devoid of all pleasures. I dreaded the day she would leave like a mad person dreading the end of the world.

The more I delved deeper into its power, the more I felt my mind turning into an empty hollow—a fearful symmetry luring me into the darkness. I quickly retreated to the reality in front of me and turned to look at the huge, embellished Christmas tree that stood near the sofa. It was a mocking antithesis of the storm brewing inside of me.

I fell into a deep reverie with the lulling sweetness of the Christmas songs emanating from the speakers. A world of my own where anything was possible.

A small cottage-like house twinkled with multicolored ferry lights, reflecting softly on the freshly fallen Christmas snow. Faint, joyful music played in the background somewhere, in one of the rooms. A half-cut velvety cake made from raisins and brown sugar rested on the round dining table. Underneath it, a poodle slumbered in her plush dog bed. On the other side of the room, a couple in their mid-sixties sat on a couch near the fireplace browsing Netflix, unable to decide what to put on but still happy figuring it out together. The lady sipped on a shake she made from vanilla and oat milk. She then picked up a piece of cake from a desk beside her, took a small bite, and offered the rest to her man. His eyes closed as he got lost in the rich flavors of the cake his lady had baked. She rested her head on his shoulder, snuggling in his blanket. He cleaned off a tiny dot of cream glued to the strawberry gloss on her lower lip. Colorful lights glistened off her smooth cheeks that retained their pink color from when she was young. He leans in to kiss her under the roof they had built together.

A change of the track in the Christmas playlist brought me back to the present.

Maya sat on a couch across me, slurping vanilla-oat milkshake while Mrs. Caul and Lalita were busy setting up food for dinner. Maya looked like a little child enjoying a delicacy for the first time. She was oblivious of how I observed the little things about her. With a heavy heart, I admired the way her soft lips touched the tip of the straw above her glass —the lips that I could only kiss in the fallacy of my reveries.

But the fact that I couldn't bring myself to tell her all about my feelings and the way she had turned my world upside down didn't stop me from cherishing the rare moments I had spent with her over a month or two. She would be in her room or out for some work with her friends on regular days. She didn't stay long enough for me to get enough of her presence in the house. Our rooms were close by, but we never visited each other. She came and went. I came and went to work too. Separate schedules and responsibilities controlled our lives. She had her worries; I had mine.

But there were days when I would meet her outside the house beside the cemetery, and I would ask her whether she would join me for a walk. She would agree, and we would talk about what had happened to us over the day. At times, she'd invite me to join her for a ride down the street to grab a quick bite. At rarer times still, she would call me for dinner with her sweet voice, freezing the blood in my veins for a moment before it could go back to function again normally.

I had no clue of how she felt when I called her name or if she ever thought of me, even once, before she retired to bed. But I was sure of this. That those moments kept me alive and breathing on my darkest nights—they were like lifeboats to me. And no matter how much I wanted it, the walls of my heart were too high to climb. I never reached the end of the tunnel. Maybe it's all my fault. Maybe I feared too much about what she would say. Maybe I had grown too comfortable with the cave inside my soul that prevented any light from entering. Maybe she was just like me. Perhaps we were just two people lost inside the prison of their minds.

Sipping on her red wine, Mrs. Caul recalled pleasant memories of past dinners when extended families hosted one big gathering where everybody shared their delicacies. The ever-growing differences among the kids changed how social events happened in modern times. While I wasn't excited imagining eating with twenty-eight other people, I knew what Mrs. Caul missed. A constant clinking of the spoons, ladles, and spatulas bespoke how much we enjoyed the food. As I finished my meal, Lalita made a revelation about the cake she baked—a plum cake with raisins and fruits to celebrate the festive season of Christmas. The end of the feast was marked by a sudden rise in turmoil as the empty utensils lay scattered on the table as a testament to the great Christmas party. I was helping Lalita wash the used utensils when Maya suddenly blurted out,

"You know, you can just use the dishwasher."

"Or maybe you should get up and help me wash them, young lady," Lalita retorted.

"I have been doing everything since morning." Maya came to her defense.

"What do you mean? I prepared everything by myself. You can't be serious," Lalita said as she stopped what she was doing and looked straight at Maya.

What started as a tease turned into something more serious, and I was right in the middle of it, clueless as to what was the wisest thing to do. I continued doing the dishes, trying to stay out of their business.

"You haven't been helpful at all, Maya. You better not tell me what to do around here."

"Oh, stop getting all worked up over a silly comment. Grow up!" Maya returned, looking visibly annoyed.

"Don't be ridiculous. You're the one who's mean here." Lalita raised her voice.

"You girls better stop being childish now," Mrs. Caul yelled from the other room.

Then gradually, their argument went from a topic that started from something silly about the dishes to a more personal one. I couldn't understand any of their angst. I had no idea what was going on between them. I stood there looking blankly at the scene, completely puzzled. The situation was getting out of hand.

"My God, Maya! Don't vent out stress from your life on me!" Lalita said in a bitter tone.

"Hey, enough! Both of you!" Mrs. Caul yelled, smashing her fist on the table. A fork yanked itself from the plate and fell on the floor. I didn't notice her coming to the kitchen, but she stood between them, looking irritated at the nuisance.
Both Maya and Lalita stopped for a few seconds. But before I could relax a bit, Lalita spoke again.

"I wish your car never reaches there and you have a hard time staying alone. That's what you want, right?" Lalita yelled, storming out of the dining hall.

Maya stood up. I saw tears gathering under her eyelids.

"Hmm…" She mumbled something under her breath and walked out without completing her sentence. I heard a loud thud. They had both slammed their doors shut with all their might.

Mrs. Caul sighed. I had never seen her do that.

"Don't mind the silly girls, Gaurav. They do that sometimes." Mrs. Caul said, looking at me with ruminating eyes as if tired of the incessant brawling of the sisters.

"Why do they have to start with their childish arguments again. That too when Maya is about to leave!" She complained, wiping the table with a wet cloth. I realized how clueless I was about their family.

"You look worried, Gaurav. Ha-ha. They'll be fine in the morning. Just leave them be." She said, smiling at me.

I nodded my head in affirmation and silently headed out to my room, lifelessly wondering about how dramatically that pleasant evening had turned into an utter fiasco. The background music that cheered up the house somehow lost its charm, turning the celebration into a dismal event. So many things perturbed me at that moment. The bitterness in their faces while they argued, the tears on Maya's face, and Mrs. Caul's reminder of Maya's departure soon. I couldn't contain it in my heart. It wanted to detonate itself from my chest. Seeing Maya cry had made me all the more pathetic. Could I ever be able to understand the troubles of her heart? Could I ever share her pain? Do I even know her? My Maya.

My head began to hurt in frustration. I couldn't decide whether I should try to go and talk to her or just go and shut myself forever in my room.

"Leave them be," Mrs. Caul had said to me before I left, but every inch of my soul wanted to crack open her door and embrace her.

As I walked past her room, I could hear her breaking into a perineal ocean of sorrow. Her silent sobs drew me closer to her, and in a trice, I felt the walls between us crumbling down in pieces. I entered and called out to her. "Maya…" There was a sudden downpour outside the house. It was odd that such a downpour could happen during winter. Tiny droplets of rain splashed through the leaking window and the ceiling. I went and sat down beside her, gently caressing her face and wiping the tears from her eyelashes while she gazed into my eyes. Her clothes were soaked in the frigid water, revealing the shape of her body. She moved in closer and placed her hands on the sides of my neck. I leaned over, embracing her, and touched her forehead with mine, my nose slightly grazing hers. I felt her body trembling along with her bated breaths. We sat there for a long time, soaked in the cold waters from the leakage. "I have to go, Gaurav," she said and kissed me. "Please stay," I implored as I broke away from her lips. A sudden touch, something colder than the rain, made me turn around. A black-feathered demon held my hand as I struggled to free myself from his grip. I looked back and saw her sitting calmly inside the floating chariot that would soon be submerged in the dense icy water that the floor had transformed into.

As the demon loomed over me, I woke up with all my might, drenched in a cold sweat. I felt my heart race painfully under my chest as though my ribs could not hold it in place.

Recurring dreams rendered me sleepless for almost a week. I tried to comprehend ways to subdue the dream, but there was no means of escape. I must be going crazy, I thought.

~~*~~

Like the steady onset of winter after the remnants of sweet autumn, the day of her cold departure came.

I was in the living room the week before when her aunt called over the phone to wish her luck. There was something in the ambiance. I watched. I watched her face. I knew then. My fists clenched on the leather of the sofa and were at the brink of damaging it. My throat closed up as I cast down my eyes to the floor and hoped nothing came out of them.

"I am going next week, Buji …" she sighed.

"Back… in May, yes," she had said in a melancholic tone.

The pain of parting overwhelmed me to the extent that I could feel my heart fragmenting into pieces inside my flimsy chest. The thought of separation caused me immense distress, and I felt myself plunging into an abyss. Deep down, I tried consoling myself that she would return, and I passed a sigh of relief at the thought of her arrival. But a sudden fear grasped me, a fear of the unknown, as I wondered if I would ever get a glimpse of her again.

Innumerable questions clouded my mind as I contemplated the different scenarios in my head.

What if she never comes back? What if I lose her? These unanswered questions slowly fed off me, and I sensed my consciousness descending into a vicious void.

The world moved on while I lay still in my bed. The commotion outside was an incongruous contrast to my mind—a self-made fictitious space that was now just barren land. The rustic furniture in my room looked pale as if empathizing with me. The colorless walls cried out in unison with my thoughts as if drowning in the nostalgia of the several separations it had endured over the years. For a moment, I felt that the house was a living entity. The walls seemed a little longer, the ceiling a little darker, the windows of my room seemed foggier than they used to. It was as though the house knew my anguish, and it was morphing itself into a dejected being to comfort me. As I observed the intricate details of the house, I could feel my soul reviving. The ache of separation was nothing in comparison to the bliss of seeing her again. A ray of hope sprouted in my soul as I jumped out of my bed to bid her farewell.

I'm going to say a proper goodbye to her. Gaurav. Stop sulking and go to her room now!

I felt my nerves jolting with a sudden dosage of determination.

Mrs. Caul dragged Maya's suitcase downstairs. She was going to help her daughter settle down in the new town. Lalita put on her shoes and grabbed her car keys.

"Come down when you're ready," she said. The sisters had settled issues between them soon after the night it happened. As much chaos their argument had created, their truce had happened without my notice. The sharp grinding sound of the zippers emerging from Maya's room made me realize that she was all set for sailing. Her door squeaked as I pushed it open.

"Maya," I asked boldly, clearing my throat.

She turned to the door and said, "Yeah?"

"Hey!" I said, walking inside the room.

"Ready to go?"

"Almost."

"How long is the flight?"

"An hour."

"Has your car reached there?"

"Yeah, delivered where I am staying." She answered without looking at me. It was the first time I got a sense of her room. It smelt just like her. I felt intoxicated by her scent that emanated from all around her room.

"I got a journal for you as a Christmas gift. It's on the dressing table." She said, pointing out at the table. My hands were on that journal before she finished her sentence.

"You got this framed?" I asked full of surprise as I noticed the photo frame on her table. I picked up the wooden frame unable to process the surge of emotions I felt as I looked at the awkward selfie she had taken when we had gone out for our first walk.

"Yeah, it was our first walk together. I am gonna take this one with me." She replied.

"I thought… I'll come… and say bye. In a proper manner." I stuttered. I had no idea where my jolt of determination to remain standing in her room came from. I wanted her to look at me for once.

I wanted to say more things to her, but I could not. She turned to me at last after she fixed her shoelaces. She had a downcast expression on her face. I didn't know how to read them. She walked to me, leaving her half-zipped suitcase on the floor, put her arms around my neck, and hugged me. There was nothing else in the world I had coveted except to be embraced by her. And it had happened to me right at the very moment.

I quickly wrapped my arms around her and felt the beating of her heart. Her hug was like a warm blanket enveloping my soul. I stood in the physical space of her room, lost in thought. My mind found it hard to process anything, and I felt the cosmos losing its symmetry as I stood there holding her in a warm embrace.

One blink of an eye, a tiny fraction of an instant, was all it took for my otherwise robust control on feelings to shatter. I breathed and gulped in a faint attempt to bury my emotions as tears brimmed in my eyes.

"I'll see you soon, Gaurav," she said.

And nothing else was needed after I heard that, for I felt as if I could wait for her on those words till infinity ran out. She broke away from my arms and left the room, taking a huge slice of my dejected heart with her.

I paced out of my room later that day and knocked at her door, hoping for an answer, but it was eerily quiet. An uncanny silence had engulfed the room, transforming it into a lifeless concrete space. There was nothing but a sense of numbness governing my heart.

~~*~~

Emptiness

I stood in the middle of a hundred shipping containers loaded with bathtubs, sinks, and other plumbing supplies. Groups of people kept rushing past me. A few forklifts crossed across the lanes; big trucks and trailers screamed while being reversed; chimneys of the nearby factories pierced the sky; there was smoke of all colors and smells of all kinds, all over. All the chaos in my workplace that I had managed to ignore, all of a sudden seemed too much to bear. Ever since Maya left, the world around me had turned against me.

The warehouse, despite being enormous, suffocated me. The noise I was well-accustomed to drilled through my skull and pierced my ears. The people I had been working with for months became strangers. The work itself that became a routine for my livelihood turned bizarre. Regardless of the bustle at my workplace, I felt empty inside.

I would check my phone several times in the hope of receiving her text but to no avail. Her silence killed me more every day. Days turned into weeks, and I could feel my hopes crushing as I thought of her being in a faraway land. I kept waiting hopelessly for her to reach out to me, but it never materialized. I had typed a hundred texts hoping I would send those to her one day, but I could never press the send button. In the end, I would only resort to a simple "Goodnight Maya." She would text me too, on rare occasions, but we never talked about our feelings. I would occasionally hear Lalita and Mrs. Caul speak with her over the phone. Whenever they did, I would stop whatever work I was doing and listen. I longed to hear her voice.

I tortured my mind into believing that she must be too busy to use her phone or chat with anyone, but she seemed to drift further and further away from me each passing day.

I skipped my lunch and instead left an hour early. I hopped on a bus, any bus, and extended myself the courtesy of having a tour of the city, six days a week, without a miss. While on the bus, I ate my lunch and listened to PropheC—one of my favorites and probably hers too. Our short rides to McDonald's had this music playing in the background. It was one of the happiest moments of my life—sitting next to her in her car. When the entire playlist ended thrice, I caught a bus back home.

~~*~~

One evening, Lalita came up to me after I had returned from work—well, kind of. I entered the kitchen to fix myself a snack while she made her smoothie.

"So, working hard lately?" She asked like a teacher to her student as she cut up a mango.

"Me? Yeah…" I moistened my throat so I could answer confidently, "…yeah."

"For 14 hours, every day?" The look in her eyes warranted that she had many more questions to ask, more like an interrogation to conduct, and the knife in her hand did not help at all.

"14?" My gaze was downcast on the floor,

"Oh..."

"Yeah. You've been coming home so late."

"They have...a lot of work for me...actually," I said and kept nodding my head, so she believed me.

"I see. How long will this continue?"

"Sorry, what...continue?"

"84-hours work week. How long will it continue?"

"Until May... no! I mean...maybe May."

"And after that?"

"After that? After that...I think they won't have much work. Yeah! They won't have much work from May." I said apparently with confidence, as my story made sense to me at least.

She briefly stared at me with a subtle smile on her face before heading upstairs. As though she had known and found what she wanted to know in my stupid replies.

The more I thought I wouldn't think about her, the more I missed her. I would recall seeing her sitting on the couch whenever I sat down to have dinner. I would relive the memory of meeting her at the party and miss her. I would feel something is missing from life and miss her. I would come across a stranger while going for work who might resemble her slightly, and the bangs of my heart would start again. Missing her never needed any reason to happen. Missing her happened whenever I inhaled a specific revering scent.

Missing her felt like I was perpetually drowning.

~~*~~

A few more weeks into adjusting my life to Maya's absence, I tricked myself into coming home on time, directly from work. Despite Mrs. Caul encouraging me to have lunch with her, I wouldn't oblige and instead worked diligently till the end of my shift. I was famished and thought of my stomach and the food in the fridge. The great force of starvation hustled me to return home that otherwise didn't offer me joy anymore. While a significant part of my brain was dedicated to missing her, the hungry barbarian part couldn't think of anything but food. I paced to the naan stop to catch the bus and wished the driver to rice it fast. I tofu ran to the house, opened the front dal, and rushed to the paneer fridge that had all the sabzi. And as I feasted on the food, the barbarian retreated, leaving more room for Maya to live an extraordinary life in my thoughts.

When I found no solace in anything outside of me after she left, I resorted to writing down my desperate thoughts in a notebook I had with me. If I could never find the courage to send my hundreds of typed messages directly to her, perhaps my notebook could contain my emotions and keep my secrets.

Every time I felt overwhelmed by my grief, love, and anger all at once, I spilled my jumbled thoughts onto a page and found some peace sedating my mind. To me, it was a form of retrospection to fathom the depth of my mind, to unravel the mystery it beholds —a key to my consciousness. One that can comprehend and heal the agony buried for several years. As I wrote, I found myself delving deeper into my consciousness to find solace within me. Writing about her liberated me as I embarked on a journey towards understanding myself inch by inch. The more I wrote about her, the more I learned about myself. Exploring her was like exploring the realms of my mind, and for a minute, I felt our souls were intertwined. I drew her closer to me as I painted her with my words, and I realized she was more than just a physical being—an effervescent, subconscious entity rooted in my soul.

There were certain weeks when I wrote about her every night. When I wanted an answer from her, I would flip a page and start a conversation with her memory. I asked her about her thoughts about me— how she saw me, what I meant to her, if I had managed to touch a tiny fraction of her infinite soul with my existence. Other nights, I would write about my frustrations. Like how she moved me into ecstasy with her embrace that day she left, yet never told me anything about what it meant.

Why did you hug me that day, Maya? Why did you frame our selfie? Why would you tie me to your heart forever but never give me the chance to understand you? Tell me, Maya. What did you mean when you took me in your arms that day? Say something.

~~*~~

Three painful months passed by without seeing her or hearing from her properly. I congratulated myself for not going into a coma. I had kept myself partially sane with the belief that she was equally enduring a hard time out there, trying to build a career for herself. Conditioning my mind to believe that took a lot of strength and energy. But somehow, I managed to do so with time without completely losing my mind. I wanted to think that I was healing from the sickness of being tortured by her memories every single day.

One magical Sunday (as I would like to call it), I decided to call her and tell her about my feelings. It was one of those days when I experienced bouts of extraordinary courage. I had no control over the risks I could take in those moments.

It's just been too long. I need to let her know, regardless of what her reaction would be. I coached myself that day.

What's the worst thing that is going to happen anyway? Either she'll accept me or reject me. If she says no, then what's going to happen? I'll cry my heart out if I have to. I'll grieve and grieve until I feel better. And then I'll move to some other place maybe, for I won't be able to face her if she rejects me. That is it? Yeah, that's the worst that could happen. Gaurav. You have to do it. No matter what.

I held my phone to my ear.

But if she says yes…? … oh fuck! I came to my usual senses, but it was too late to cancel the call.

Don't pick up!

Don't pick up!

Don't…

"Hey!" She spoke.

"Hey…hello Maya?"

"Yeah?" Her soft voice rang in my ears. I almost felt like crying. I had missed it so much.

"Hi," I said.

"Hi, Gaurav. How are you?" She asked me first in a very casual tone. It was as though she was talking with an old classmate.

"I'm okay, Maya. How have you been?"

"I am okay. Keeping myself busy at work."

"Congratulations! We made…you made it so far."

"Yeah, thanks… hehe…almost there." She replied.

Now's your chance! Tell her, Gaurav! Tell her everything!

"So…Maya, what's living there like?"

She paused for a little while before speaking again.

"It's just a small town. Nothing much to do." She seemed to be in a hurry. I heard noises over the phone, which made me understand that she was out somewhere important.

"Made any friends?" I asked. I knew that I was wasting precious opportunities, but I wanted to talk to her a little more. Just her voice was enough to heal me at that moment.

"Yeah, a few…" she replied. "Hey, Gaurav…?"

"Yes, Maya…?"

"Should we talk later? I am on my way to do an important assignment," she said in hurried breaths. She seemed to be walking fast.

"Oh! Okay sure. We can talk later when you're free."

"Alright. Sorry, Gaurav. Bye-bye!"

"Bye!"

My heart sank in disappointment.

If we weren't too busy, I would have told her. Yeah, I totally would have. I lied to myself.

I knew that it was simply an easy and convenient thought made up inside my head to save myself from fear and embarrassment.

Hearing her voice once again gave me all the energy I needed. Regardless of our short conversation and her hurried replies, I still reveled in the fact that she picked up my call even when she was busy.

I headed home early from work that day. I replayed her voice in my head all afternoon as I laid down on my bed in a trance-like state.

With my newly gained confidence, I was struck with another idea. If the phone call didn't work out, perhaps something else could. I thought. I got up from bed in a jiffy and rushed downstairs.

"Where are you headed now?" Lalita asked.

"Just to meet a friend."

"I didn't know you liked meeting your friends," she looked at me with her raised eyebrows, "or if you had any in the first place."

"Wow! Lalita, truer words could not have been spoken. Thank you." I said, returning her tease.

I left the house in a flash with a grand idea in my head.

~~*~~

I arrived at the entrance of a 7-ELEVEN store —an odd place to be for me. I walked into a stew of a zoo.

After crossing a swarm of stinky people, I reached where I needed to be, hoping there would be civility in that part of the zoo, but that day wasn't my day at all. A few wild-eyed junkies lined up ahead of me and a lot more older women behind me, giggling like lovestruck teens. I wondered why junkies would line up at a post office. Who were they writing to? Their supplier? And right then, the first one asked for a whitener. He stepped out of line as he got one, sniffing it, and his platoon followed. So, whiteners were the new fashion to get high in town. What was next, glue sticks?

"Next in line!" the cashier said, pointing her finger toward me as if I wasn't going to know I was the next person.

"Hey! I am here to get a postcard."

"We're out of those."

"I need to send a letter."

"Here. Prepaid stamps. Put them on the envelope and bam! How many?"

"One stamp and an envelope."

"Three dollars, fifty."

"Here."

"Receipt?"

"No, thanks!"

"Next in line…"

"Sorry, can I also borrow your pen for a minute? And a piece of paper…"
Vertical wrinkles stretched between her eyebrows, and her eyes squinted slightly.

…please?"

"You want to write your letter here? Like… right now?"

"Yes, if I may. It's kind of urgent."

"Ohkay! I use my phone for urgent matters. Just saying!"

"Believe me; I tried that."

She tossed a pen at the counter and yanked out a piece of paper.

"Thank you so much!"

"Yeah! Step aside, let me help others. You can write here," she said, pointing to a desk just beside her.

"I appreciate it."

I looked back, stepping aside. The line that had gotten to the door collectively gave me the most intimidating look ever.

"Tell me when you're done. Don't worry about the line," she said, grinning a little.

"You are so kind!"

"Yeah, you bet."

With my tongue between my teeth, I began to write:

Hey! Maya,

It's me, Gaurav.

~~I hope you didn't get late for the assignment. I know how much effort goes into being punctual. If you got late because of my call, I am sorry.~~

You spent more than three months there, all by yourself, in that remote town. I am proud of you. Kudos to you on making it so far so good, and I hope you will tread through the remaining time like a boss.

~~There is also something I want to tell you about. You deserve to know it from me in person, but I don't have the courage for that yet. And I owe you the truth.~~

~~It all started when I first saw you at Mrs. Caul's birthday party. I just want you to know that you are the~~

~~I would like to spend the rest of my lif~~ ~~I am way past the stage of just likin~~

I put the pen down and sealed the envelope.

"Hey! I am done," I said, extending the letter to where she stood.

"Great. Who would it go to?"

"To Maya!"

"And where?"

"To the town, she has gone to."

"Exactly!"

We both stood at either side of the counter, staring at each other, competing to see who blinked first. She must have thought I was an idiot like I felt she was.

"Sir, this letter isn't going to fly to your Maya by itself..." Brutal sarcasm was evident in her tone, "...write an address."

"Fu… sorry. Yeah! The address…right!"

"You there?" I typed into my phone. My eyes bled as I stared at the space below my text. I saw that she was online.

"Yeah?"

"What's your address?"

"Why?"

"I wanted to send you something."

"Like what?"

"It's a surprise!"

"I don't really like surprises."

"You don't? Oh…okay."

"Boss! You got it?" the cashier asked, wagging the sealed blank envelope.

What should I have told her? That my beloved didn't like surprises? Or she didn't want one from me? Or didn't even like me?

I walked to her and took the envelope, and said, "Never mind. Thank you!" I waved goodbye at her like a fallen warrior. Then before another group of junkies walking toward the store could enter, I exited.

I took a walk back home, wondering how exceptionally mighty Maya was, for her minuscule actions had a profound impact on me.

Maya wouldn't be an extraordinary girl if she didn't also have the power to easily break my otherwise unconquered heart, clog my lungs, and cripple my brain with her texts or sometimes the lack of it. Little did she know that for every beating my heart took when it failed at connecting with her, it got back up stronger. The fidelity I had for her didn't fill my heart but made it ever bigger such that it constantly had some room for heartbreaks. I was getting better at fitting her rejections into my day. How lucky I was to have a stellar person like Maya in my life—someone whose ignorance towards me worked wonders. I could not fathom what miracles her attention to me would have spun. Was she even born or made or just happened in the world like magic? As the tsunami of thoughts about her ravaged my mind, my eyes got stuck at the path I was walking on.

The sidewalk across the suburb was made of cement and fine gravel. It had several slabs aligned with each other as though a puzzle got all its pieces right. I covered one slab in one stride and a half, sometimes two, when the wind blew hard against me. Quite a few times, its solid surface melted like wax. And then the tip of the runners I wore caught a few drops of water when I strolled, but there wasn't a trace of rain for miles.

My strange adventures that day tired me to the bones, and I slept peacefully that night with the memory of her sweet voice I had heard that day, after what seemed like ages.

~~*~~

The remaining days turned into weeks, and the anticipation of her arrival seemed to grow heavier each day. The very thought of having a glimpse of her gave me a tingling sensation, and an emotional paradox of loss and hope overwhelmed me. I would sometimes decide to call sick at work if it weren't for my partner, who was entirely dependent on me. Often, I found myself lost in a reverie, which delayed my work. It was almost like time was contracting, months shortening into days, days into minutes as I felt time fleeting away while I dreamed of her. The wait seemed never-ending, but I had learned to embrace it with time. Lazy showers had turned into a reviving experience. The intense sweet aroma of the foamy shower gel was reminiscent of the fragrance that enveloped Maya's body. Washing with warm water was a meditation for the senses that reminded me of Maya's hug. I felt her warmth growing inside and, in a minute, the distance seemed like an illusion —a faint hope, a mirage to my parched soul.

Mundane Sundays morphed into beautiful days, drawing me closer to the day of her arrival. Weekend morning breakfasts looked like a feast celebrating the memories of the effervescent soul, a salient persona that had graced the house for years. The chapped colorless walls had brightened as if flushing at the thought of a reunion with a long-lost lover. I felt my withered soul spring back to life like a Lazarus rising from ashes as I looked around. Days passed by, finally leading me to the most awaited moment—the moment of her arrival. It was finally the month of May. Every morning, I would wait impatiently, hoping to see her unload the luggage from the back of her car through the small dusty window in my room. One fine morning I found Mrs. Caul preparing Maya's room which renewed my hope of her arrival. Lost in the maze of a dream, I felt Maya embark on a journey, carrying along with her the warmth of the summer sun.

~~*~~

I had been so caught up weaving different scenarios about the day she would return, constructing scenes of our hugs and kisses, that I could not believe just how far I had come. On any other Sunday in her absence, I would have not gotten out of bed until 10 am in the morning. I would have worn my pajamas and T-shirt all day long, not caring about my dishevelled look. But not that day. On that day, I woke up early as soon as my alarm clock rang, took a shower and put on the same athleisure outfit she liked from our first walk. Quite similar to how a temple priest prepares for his prayer to the divine, I was more than eager to see my Maya after five months that felt like an eternity to me. I'm not trying to be dramatic but I had missed her terribly. I wondered if her hair was longer now, if she thought about me half as much as I thought about her…

Mrs. Caul had gone to attend a Gurudwara ceremony. Likewise, Lalita had left to meet with her friends later that morning. It wasn't the first time I was home by myself, but the realization of being alone in the house registered for the first time, inducing several waves of contemplations inside my mind, or perhaps stomach I am not so sure. Little did I know that I would soon experience the oomph of being there all by myself.

How am I supposed to receive her? How would she react after seeing me after so many months? Could she probably be as excited as me? Would we hug? Oh! Certainly… Kiss? Shit! Why is there a strange sensation in my stomach that feels awfully familiar? As I surpassed the ordinary standards of overthinking, I heard the garage door opening and immediately ran downstairs to look at the security monitor that in itself was an adventurous act on my part. Once her car was parked, I reached up the door ledge, eyes wide, hoping to catch the sight of her figure as she made her way towards the house. I had imagined a hundred times how my chest would bustle with sheer joy upon finally seeing her after all this time but the excitement I felt as my eyes followed her elegant for, was unlike anything I had felt before. I pounced and bounced and ran as if intoxicated by the explosion in my brain. Before she would ring the doorbell, I took a step outside.

As she gazed at me, she stepped back slowly. Her inspection probably lasted for a few seconds, but it seemed like it took forever. Suddenly, the air between us crackled and I wished to move closer to her to close the gap between us. But for some reason, I couldn't move my feet. I just froze as I stared at her. Her eyes lingered on on my lips for a moment and then as she looked straight into my eyes, I finally moved. It was inevitable. A tempest built in those damnable eyes sucked me in like a moth to a flame. Her arms wrapped around my neck gave me enough spark to compensate for the dark I had been in for months. As soon as there was some space between our chests, she hugged me again. That would have given her eyes the time it needed to let go of the tears they held.

~~*~~

For a few weeks after she had arrived, tales of her bravery echoed in the house. Every now and then, she would narrate one of the incidents that had occurred, and in no time, I found myself lost in her words. One fine Sunday morning when I was preparing my blueberry shake, I could hear her narrating an incident to Mrs. Caul and Lalita, and I overheard as she spoke,

"Winters had just passed, and it was the month of March when one day, as dawn broke, I drove my car to work. I worked for a natural resource company, and their site was up in the mountains. As I entered the trails, I saw a million pine trees, shrubberies, and egg-shaped rocks on either side of the swiveled road. Although I had been driving on that path for a few months, the quietness of the empty trail was eating me up on that particular day. I had a bad vibe about it. If anything were to happen to me there, it wasn't until evening that people coming back from the site to the valley would notice me. I couldn't even call anyone because the network only worked in the valley or up the mountain. I drove for about fifteen minutes and was in the middle of nowhere when I saw two giant black bears blocking the road. I had to stop my car. I had heard stories from my colleagues about bears attacking people in that area, so all I could imagine was being bitten and killed by those beasts. Then I realized I was in the car, and if there was any threat to my life, I could just push hard on the accelerator. But that was easier thought than done.

One of them saw me and decided it hated me on sight. It walked right by my window, eyeing me the whole time. Streaks of saliva endlessly fell from its mouth. I could hear it breathing and its nostrils pumping. It might have been the size of my car, probably a bit smaller, but heavier than the car for sure. The way it looked at me, we both knew who dominated the land. I had never experienced that kind of terror in my life. Time slowed down or maybe not; I didn't care. All I could think of was those animals breaking the glass of my window or the windshield and attacking me. One swing of their paws could easily puncture the tires. And then I would be just stuck there, waiting for death to come. It strolled around the car and went to the other one that hadn't moved at all since I arrived. And then they both disappeared into the woods. I cruised to the worksite without worrying about any speed limit and thought of returning to Vancouver quite a few times. Bwahaha..." She finished telling one of her several stories of bear encounters in the jungles of the hills.

When she narrated, I got a fair chance to look at her glowing face. The sheer charm of her voice worked its way up from the core to the fingertips. I had been longing to hear her and to see her to the content of my heart. Perhaps, that was why I looked forward to listening to her adventures in the remote town.

Scary episodes of her car skidding on the snowy roads and events where she had to tread on foot for miles in the dark to get help whenever her car stuck in the snow kept me on the hook. She drove for eight hours on unknown, dangerous terrains on her way back to Vancouver. What could have been more daring than that? Maya was a warrior who pulled out victories from the jaws of defeat.

~~*~~

The day had drained me physically, but I failed to sleep. The more I tried, the more I wound up contemplating about her. Several questions clouded my mind, and the urge to fight my thoughts was suddenly lost. I lay in bed, looking straight at the ceiling, conjuring up a fantasy world. One in which I am a successful author—something I had dreamed of as a child. The stark white color of the ceiling and the soft rhythmic ticking of the clock made me drowsy, and in no time, I was lost in a trance, a labyrinth devised by my imagination. My thoughts merged with my dream, and I had a vision I wished I could turn into reality.

The bookstore drowned in a sea of people, children, and adults swimming in it alike. Each opening of the door brought more customers in. Weekends were the prime days for the businesses in downtown Vancouver. So, when they had just opened in the morning, I arrived to make arrangements for the big event. A rectangular desk covered with a navy-blue sheet bearing the store's logo was set up in the events section. The store manager was kind enough to beautifully arrange a stack of books, a few gel pens, and a water bottle on it. The chair they gave me was comfortable to sit in, though I was too excited to remain sitting. Getting along with the gloomy days when Maya was gone left me with a poetry book I wrote, and it was its launch that day. They had also put up a few posters with my book's cover on the walls and sales counter.

Waves of readers passed by me. They were tagging along their small children. Some were dragging strollers with babies sleeping in them, and others just strolled around the aisles. A few came to my table and smiled, congratulating me for the feat. They picked my book, read the blurb, and then flicked through the pages while I tried to jack up my stress response. A few asked me to sign it, and fewer took photos with me, giving me a semi-celebrity feel. Amidst the laughter, the chatter, the excitement, and the bustle, my eyes were fixed on the door with hopes to see someone special enter. Each time someone came in, my gut twisted, and my heart fell to my feet. She said she might come, and that was reason enough for me to stare at the door like a fanatic. And the moment she arrived, everything… A rush of blood in my ears and head woke me up. The reverberating chaos became a cool, silent breeze.

No matter what Maya wore, the colors on her clothes sprang to life. Colors were mere purposeless, dejected pigments when not worn on her body. My senses were no better than that of a drunkard whenever she put on black. I would be safe at home where I had my room to hide and a bed to fall back in admiration, but who was there to get hold of me? The black V-neck T-shirt she wore revealed the delicate line of her collarbone just above the neckline that I had imagined kissing so reverently that a hundred real kisses wouldn't have matched its verve. Her snow-white skin could even enchant the newborn daisy petals. I wasn't sure about the existence of God but hugging Maya was the closest I had ever been to divinity. I needed no more book signings, no photographs with anyone, and nothing else, for who I needed had arrived.

"Hey! You came," I exclaimed.

"Yeah…it's my first time at such an event."

If we could experience a whole life together for the first time...

"Me too," I said, unable to hide the joy in my voice.

"A signed copy for me, please?" She teased me.

"Oh! C'mon. The author is going home with you." We laughed.

My phone buzzed all of a sudden, waking me up from a deep slumber. I looked at my watch, which read 8:30 A.M.

Glowing streaks of yellow light around the edges of Maya's door pierced through my eyelids that only moments ago held darkness on otherwise bright days. Those fascinating rays turned the entrance of her room into a gateway to the magical world. A mild clatter of the drawers, running taps in the bathroom, and thuds on the desk foretold how she got ready to work from home, at dawn, every weekday. She looked in the mirror atop the dressing table, poised, with an eternal sense of discipline, and held a brush like an artist expressing herself on her skin—a fresh canvas every morning. She wouldn't have made any difference by applying lipstick on her slender, rosy lips, so she used a strawberry Chapstick instead. Then she slightly leaned in for a closer look and pulled on the bottom lid of her left eye to put kohl eyeliner. Her art set her up for the day ahead. She preferred a reasonably natural look, for she owned her self-worth. Beauty lay in the beheld in that room because the beholder was awestruck, unable to process anything. Maya then sat in a chair and opened a laptop, in the same way from when I stood outside the house. As her drumming fingers stroked on the keyboard, my little brain reminded me of my business. And my mind sneaked out through the shut door without her knowing.

~~*~~

Reunion

It was a bright Sunday morning and the house bustled with the chatter, cheers, and irresistible smell of warm food and caramelized desserts. On a couple of occasions after May, people of all generations came by the dozens. Guests my age walked around in the hall and kitchen, bagging chips and popcorns and doughnuts from the bowls glued to the sticky surface of the quartz countertops. Steady traffic befell the fridge as they grabbed their drinks. Some sat on the stairs holding cans and bottles of pop and beer in their hands. Some hung out in doorways. Maya's cousins were a mix of funky and smart boys and girls.

When her mellow laugh fell in my ears, dispersing all the cackles echoing around, I stood idle wherever I was walking while my eyes ran searching for her. There she was, sitting among them at the dining table, chit-chatting and rolling a streak of her hair with a finger. Subtle movements of her head, slight shrugs of her shoulders, and sweet smiles on her lips blew life into the conversations.

I was aware of the rigor I endured during those celebrations. And because the rapture my heart tasted from seeing her laugh, hug, and taking photos outweighed the rupture it sustained for not being a part of it all, I stayed downstairs.

Being suspicious of everyone present, I dared to peek at the most precious face ever. And as I caught a glimpse, my gaze betrayed me and refused to lower down. In that awakening moment, I realized how dramatically the more time I spent in her vicinity, the lesser it seemed. I had been filling her in my eyes forever, and yet every time, it was the first time I saw her. I had known her for years, yet I knew her only in the moments she appeared before me. How closely aware I was of her laughs and sobs, smiles and frowns, work and rest, stress and comfort, fears and nerves and everything in between, and yet how dangerously clueless I was.

"If we could talk when we need to and about whatever. If we could pour our hearts out to each other. If we could go on walks and car rides. If we went eating out together and on dieting. If we listened to each other, wiped each other's tears, made each other laugh, hugged and kissed each other, and sometimes fought a little!

If we had a bond that went beyond the body, mind, and soul. If we spent the rest of our lives together and celebrated Christmas as I envisioned once, and then maybe after watching you sleep and waking up for two more decades after 2065 and loving you every day, I died with no regrets…"

I sat at the table with Maya, talking to her, but nothing came out of my mouth.

~~*~~

The Chaos

An Indian restaurant on a Sunday evening wasn't the best place for an introvert, yet I found myself entering one. A smartly dressed waitress greeted me with an ear-to-ear smile. Another with a platter of paneer tikka rushed by me as I went further inside. My eyes followed her, and before my feet marched towards the crispy-soft nuggets gracing someone else's table, I turned my head in search of Kev. All calls of duties were tough, but friends' calling was more potent than the rest.

"Wassup! Bro," he hollered, waving at me from a distance. I weaved my way through the crowds of guests and cocktail-bearing waiters.

"Hey! How have you been?" I asked, pulling a chair for myself.

"Nothing new, Gaurav. Old, same old."

"And yet I am ten miles away from my home with you. I better get a life!"

"Bwahaha!" His beefy body that hadn't changed a bit in the last two years plumped up and down. Only when I saw his face again after so long, I realized how much I had missed his company. We had grown apart since I left for Victoria. But he had always been in my thoughts.

A waitress attended us with a pen and notepad in her hands.

"Hey! Guys, ready to order?" She asked.

"One Caesar salad, please."

"And cold water...what do you want?" He asked me.

"One paneer tikka, and that would be all. And just water."

"On your table in five. Thank you!" She glided away.

"It's been so long, and you never even called." He commented.

"Work was hectic," I said in utter guilt because I had purposefully ignored his calls at times.

"Is that even a valid reason?"

"And I was busy applying for law enforcement jobs."

"Here's iced water for you, gentlemen."

"Thank you!" Both of us said.

"Anyway, what's bothering you?" I asked. Something was going on, or he wouldn't have asked to meet me.

"My girlfriend is insisting on getting married."

"Yeah, so?"

"Here's your salad and paneer tikka. Enjoy!" She was gone even before I could take my eyes off the sizzling paneer.

"I am not ready for that kind of commitment." He whimpered.

"Do you love her?"

"Yes."

"Be real."

"Of course!" He asserted.

"Then count it as your blessing that your love wants to marry you. It's the most wonderful thing that could happen to anyone. Unfortunately, not everyone is lucky enough to afford this luxury."

"I don't know, man. It's frustrating sometimes."

"Are you for real? You know what's frustrating?"

"What?" He asked.

Ripples emerged in the water as I picked up my glass. After I chugged half of it, I wedged my fork in a cube of paneer.

"What?" He barked.

"Not seeing your beloved is frustrating and seeing them briefly too. Being unable to talk to them is frustrating and having to have small talks. Loving them with your whole life while they have no idea how it revolves around them is frustrating. Laughing and crying when they do, yet not with them, is frustrating. Eating at the same time yet not at the same table is frustrating. Sleeping at the same time yet not in one bed is frustrating. Staying with them in their house and being unable to tell them you want to be with them for the rest of your life is frustrating. Meeting your world every fucking day and realizing you aren't a part of it is frustrating. Having their door next to yours and yet being unable to walk through it is frustrating. And not just that, caring about their car, their laptop, their phone, even the door and room and..."

People at the nearby tables stared at me. All eating and chit-chat paused there.

"…is frustrating." I tilted my head down, glancing at my plate. The fork annihilated the nugget it was jammed in, so much so that it couldn't be picked up. So, I used a spoon.

"Dayum!" He yelped, quickly muffling his mouth with the napkin.

"O…M…G! Maya!" He whispered.

I shivered at the realization of having given it away. There was no going back from there.

"How could you be so sure? It could have been Lalita." I enquired.

"Bwahaha…He-he-he…he-he…" He snorted.

I raised my eyebrows in curiosity. "Lalita is my girlfriend," he said.

"Okay…What? What???"

"Yeah, man. It's been a while. When I stayed at her house, we had a thing going on." He asserted.

"Oh! My… that's why she was so eager to see our basement that hot summer day. I should have realized from the way you both hugged each other…" I was surprisedly connecting the dots, "…and the flirting."

"You can't marry Lalita… if you're not a hundred percent sure, okay?" I became defensive suddenly.

"She is a wonderful girl. You understand?" I asserted.

"Of course, she is. You think I don't know that?" He laughed heartily.

"You got to tell Maya about it. Tonight!" He commanded.

"Woah!"

"You tell her, or I will."

"Hey! Please, do not. I will, soon."

"Okay."

"Okay then. See you!"

I got up from the table and shook hands with him. As I stepped out of the door, an unpleasant twist in my gut expanded to my chest. The deal wasn't sealed yet. I turned around.

"Do I have your word, man to man?"

He stared at me in confusion. "You will not tell Maya," I said.

"You have my word, bro! A man to a man."

I walked home that night wondering how I got off two stops further, despite being wide awake through the ride.

~~*~~

The dark sky wailed, and thunder rumbled in heaping waves, sobbing at the occasion of my heartsore departure. The room that gave me warmth and comfort will welcome others now. The walls and roof that protected me will shield others. I folded my clothes, putting them in a bag, and chanced upon the sobbing mirror. It feared getting dusty and forlorn again and stared at me in hopes of assurance that it would be alright. I kept myself busy, stuffing clothes in my bag and packing a carton with gifts, souvenirs and cards from the family and pretended I never saw it weep but ignoring it became hard when tears rolled down its eyes. I braced my susceptibility to the uncertain future and answered it in the affirmative.

Most of the appliances and furniture were already on their way to Mrs. Caul's downsized house in the outskirts of the same city. The family moved out the following week after I left the house that had been an ardent companion to my silent adventures for the past year and a half. When opening the giant front door, flashbacks of doing so for the first time came rushing to my gut, and it somersaulted the same way it did then. But the direction towards which I was headed was opposite. I stood at the jamb of the door and looked upstairs to Maya's room for the last time and, despite just seeing her a minute ago, sneaked in again without her knowing.

"Hey!" I called out to her.

"Hmm..." she replied, and then words became uncalled-for.

Her hug was stronger than anything I had ever experienced. Since there was still some room to breathe, I squeezed her again so she couldn't see my damp eyes. Damp eyes? Oh! The mirror never cried, I thought to myself. I heard her rapid breaths and caught her zesty fragrance and fell for her once again, and promised her so much more than what I had in the last two years.

"I'll text you when I want to hang out with you." I sort of mandated it, but she must seal the deal.

"Okay?" I asked.

"Hmm…" She nodded as her chin touched my shoulder two times up and down, and then I let go of my hug. Before my mind changed and I stayed there for one more night and then another one and another one, I walked out of her room.

Back at the door, the downpour washed everything anew. I darted towards my newly bought car—the same model, color, and everything as Maya's car, yet nothing like it, and plunked my luggage in its trunk. I was drenched to the skin when I sat in the driver's seat.

"This night is the beginning of a new dawn with her," I said to my car. It revved up and hurried to a nearby high-rise apartment that I rented in reply.

~~*~~

It was getting increasingly difficult to write. I stared at the blank pages in front of me, the pen felt heavy in my fingers today. I knew what I wanted to write yet let the world linger in my head. The pen had enough ink and yet it refused to bleed on the pages. Suddenly, the words that were etched on the page began to melt. Then the air felt too thick to breathe. It was the dampness on that last page that snapped me back to reality. In that moment, I realized Maya's journal had served its true purpose. Then the words flowed organically, one after another. Before I put on my uniform and left my apartment for the night shift, I wondered how long it would be before history recorded the existence of those pages. I was amazed at the achievement of writing so much in a single day —only a force as strong as love could have made me do that.

~~*~~

A hollow concrete cube made up of nothing but damp grey walls crumbled on me. Water dripping inside through its decaying roof turned the cement floor into a slippery slab of ice. A small, barred window barely permitted the fresh air in, as if it needed an appointment to visit the dungeon. No matter the weather outside, the inside of the jail always shed tears. A prison door guarded cells on either side of the narrow passageway with one way out—eight feet high, six inches thick cranky mass of steel, devoid of any aesthetics but with plenty of hopelessness. I sat at the far corner of the doorway at a wooden table that stank of mold. A dimly lit bulb hung above my head, giving me just enough light to locate some keys on the board. Rookies got pushed into a solitary block. And minutes after my night shift began, a scream pierced my brain. No one was supposed to be there. Then who could have howled? I got up to look around and what lay on the floor inside a coffin-like cell shook me, and I held its bars to keep myself from falling. As I paced to grab the key, a fire alarm caused chaos, and Maya screamed louder and for longer. I opened the lock with my trembling hands, carried her in my arms, and sprinted until I was out of my breath. When I opened the door, I saw the number 39 at the end of the hallway. 39? I was perplexed. Then I clasped the pillow I brought with me when I bolted out. Where... was I?

~~*~~

I finally entered a law enforcement career, but it came at the price of losing my appetite and my sleep. It had been a few struggling weeks since I joined a provincial prison as a correctional officer. I worked four days on, four days off, with ten to twelve-hour rotating shifts indoors in a noisy, sticky, and hot environment. Some inmates had committed mistakes in the heat of the moment and regretted doing that. And then there was the majority with no shame, no remorse in their eyes. They were ready to do it again. I monitored and controlled that bunch of pedophiles, rapists, and murderers. Hardly any shift went by without witnessing gang fights, stabbing, seizure of contraband, or reporting tampering with the property. It was a job where I wished for my shifts to be as dull as they could be because boredom in the jail assured the safety of my life, which differed from the life outside of its despairing walls. There wasn't any peaceful day ever in that job which made the frequent nightmares I was experiencing make perfect sense. Spending time on my balcony, gazing at the breathtaking view of the city, the sky, the sea, and the mountains from the 39th floor returned the peace I lost during work, but that lasted only for so long.

It was during those hopeless days that I lay in my bed one Sunday morning, relaxed as it was my day off, and realized how important it was to confess my love to Maya and how precious time was. It took me twenty-five years to feel like that. I couldn't have afforded to wait any longer to tell her. The strange awkwardness that was there when I stayed in her house was absent since I came to my apartment. And she had sealed the deal of meeting me when I wanted to hang out with her. There could never be a better time than that Sunday to meet up with her. So, I picked up my phone and texted her.

"Hey!" I said and waited impatiently, peeking continuously at my screen now and then. After a few minutes that seemed like a few hours, my screen flashed with her name.

"Hey!" She texted.

"Done with vacuuming your room?" I asked, being well aware of her Sunday routine.

"HAHA… just now," she said.

"Any plans for the evening?"

"None so far." She confirmed.

"Want to meet up?" I gathered my courage and felt lost in the number of possible replies. A stream of blood gushed through my veins as I impatiently waited for her response.

My phone buzzed a few minutes later, and I jumped to take a look. I heard the cracking of a China dish but didn't bother to look. I knew which one had fallen—I wanted to get rid of it anyway. It was my brother calling.

"Bro, are you okay?" He asked even before I could say, "Hello."

"Why would I not be?"

"I don't know. You've been ignoring my calls. You have stopped calling Maa too." He said. He was just being himself—an annoying little brother.

"Hold on a second!" I interrupted as I saw Maya's text popping on my screen.

"Yeah! Let's meet up," she replied. "Wanna come to the Central Park for a walk?"

"Sure. What time?"

"Sorry, I got an important text. I...I have been busy lately, so I couldn't talk to Maa," I zoned back into my previous conversation.

"Busy lately? You used to talk to us almost every day. Then it became every few weeks, and now it's been months since you've called us. What is happening to you? Are you going into depression?" He asked.

"Oh! Shut up. I am fine," I assured him.

"Are you...Look, the brother I once knew was a lot different and better than this version. Although he sucked at socializing, he was the best, the coolest, and the smartest person in this whole wide world. And anyone would be lucky to be friends with him. But I feel like ever since you left for Canada, just existing in a new place, amongst new people, became taxing for you. You lost yourself somewhere between fighting these emotional battles and making peace with the chaos within. I want my brother back. I don't know what you are going through, but I know you are a warrior. Nobody made you one, so no one can take that from you." He said in a serious tone.

"Hello?"

"I...I am listening." I was caught off-guard by Aman's remark.

"Do you need me to be there? I can come in our nice big car to Canada." He tried to lighten the mood.

"He-he! I will be fine."

"Oh! I am sure you will be. You always make everything alright in the end."

And just then, Maya's text flashed. "See you at 5," it said.

"I'll call Maa tomorrow. I've got some cleaning up to do right now. Will talk later, bye!" I assured him.

"Bye!" He said, and I hung up.

The tiles on the floor of my high-rise apartment had tiny embossed dashes that registered their nominal presence when touched. And as I picked up shattered pieces of the China dish, my brother's comments, disregarding the dramatic flair, struck somewhere deep within my heart. What had been happening to me? Where was I lost? I lay on my bed wondering about my life before and after I knew her and that I would get up soon to meet her.

~~*~~

I put on my running gear when the clock ticked 4:30, took my phone, and headed down in the elevator that, to my surprise, arrived on my floor instantly. Is today my lucky day? I thought to myself. As soon as its door slid open to the ground floor and I stepped out of it, a slight disappointment took over and diminished gradually. I had forgotten to take my backpack with the package and a bottle of water, just in case Maya needed it. I might have pressed the up button ten times, only to realize it won't make any difference. The lift would take its time to reach me again. And then I realized perhaps the only frustrating thing about living in a high-rise apartment was waiting for the elevator and that it might not be my lucky day.

I rushed out of the building's main door and picked up my pace, almost running towards the park. I could have taken my car, but I needed the run. It always took my mind to somewhere unknown, in the void, and still somehow brought me back into the moment—like how I felt during a good game of chess with Mrs. Caul. My mind swarmed with questions. Is my life going to be perfect now? Or…will it leave a deep scar in my heart? For a split second, my eyes watered at the thought of the latter. Or maybe that was just the gust since I jetted to my destination.

I took the running trail of the park that was her usual walking route and hoped I would catch her soon. It had only been a minute of jogging when I saw a girl of her height and shape briskly walking afar. I zoomed under the shades of trees and found her green baseball cap merging with the flora around her. The black yoga pants she wore matched her runners. As the distance between us kept decreasing, her style and the strong pull of high voltage became prominent. Her long hair was enough for me to know it was Maya, and as soon as I was near enough, a familiar zesty fragrance entered my lungs. I needed no further indication. Her scent was enough for me to follow her with my eyes closed. As I tapped on her shoulder from behind, she shook her head, taking out the Air Pods from her ears.

"Oh, Gaurav!" She exclaimed.

"Hey!" I managed to speak up while my heart was ready to beat out of my chest, and my lungs reached the brink of exploding.

"You came here running?" She asked, surprised.

"Yeah! You need water?" I asked her and reached for my backpack before she could say anything.

"No, I am okay. I think you need it more than anyone." She said, laughing.

"No, I should wait for some time."

"How is your new job at the jail going?"

"It is going okay. I am still adjusting to the weird environment," I confessed.

"Yeah! I wonder how you're able to cope with all the stress." She commented.

"I would rather work with inmates than attend virtual meetings for hours and hours." As soon as I replied, she laughed, sensing my sarcasm aimed at her job.

"How have you been, Maya?" I asked.

"I am okay. Just settling into the new house and getting familiar with the neighborhood." She replied.

"How are Lalita and Mrs. Caul? Have they settled into the new house well?" I asked.

"They are good. I guess they find it easier to adapt to the new setting than me." She admitted.

"Do you want to sit?" I asked her as we approached a vacant bench.

"Umm…sure!" She said, and we sat on the bench that was surprisingly less warm than I had expected it to be on that hot sunny evening. I put my backpack on the ground.

"So, is anything new happening in your life?" She asked.

"I wanted to meet because it has been a long time since we last met. And I have something I need to tell you."

"Like what?" Her eyes stared at my face for the longest duration ever, waiting for me to say something. I leaned down, took out the bottle from my bag, and gulped some water. I wasn't thirsty, but I needed one last moment for that push and daring to come over me, and it did.

"Ever since I saw you first, I have been repressing my feelings for you. And I can't keep doing that anymore…"

As I uttered those words, putting my bottle in the backpack, the corner of her eyes crinkled. I continued,

"…I am not sure if you wanted it to be this way, but you must allow me to tell you the truth. I am in love with you, Maya. Probably before I even realized what love was. I was making sure it was love, and I was afraid to tell you it was, for I feared you would… I don't know…abandon me after knowing that, or worse, hate me for the rest of your life. I tried telling you during so many instances…"

"Then why didn't you?" My heart jumped out of my chest as her voice trembled on her slender strawberry lips.

"What could I have told you…"

My voice broke, and I felt my eyes getting blurry.

"That it is you who I think of every morning even before I open my eyes? Or that there hasn't been a single night where the elegance of your face didn't accompany me to my sleep? Or that I was lost the moment you came into my life? Or that I counted having you around, watching you grow as a blessing. Or that emotions are all I have, and I have you in my heart. You are every emotion I have? Or that ever since I saw you, my life came to a halt, and at the same time, it got its momentum? Or that the only place I want to be is beside you, with you? Or that you are dearer to my heart than anyone ever could be in the nearly three decades of my life?" I bent down to get my backpack again.

"There is so much to say, Maya. I did not know where to start or how to say it all. Here..." I took out an envelope from the bag and noticed my shaking hands while giving it to her. And as she opened it and held the paper, I saw her hands were shaking too. "I tried sending it to you when you were gone, but the cashier didn't let me write it properly. And I didn't even have your address..." I chuckled, recalling that experience. Her eyes opened wide as she perhaps remembered my text asking for her address that day. She then looked at me and said with a quavering voice, "I couldn't believe it when just two days ago, I heard about how you feel for me..."

"You knew? How?"

I was confused. And before she could say anything, I exclaimed, "That idiot gave me his word, man to man, that he will not share it with you. How could he..."

"No, Kev kept his promise to you. Lalita told me..." She stared at the letter again, "Kev told Lalita, not me." I had never been so out of thoughts before.

"Maya, look at me," I said, and she lifted her head. "You didn't do anything about it?" I asked.

"I... I didn't know what to do, Gaurav. I have had a bad experience with a guy in college. I was scared." Her voice stuttered. I knew if I asked any further questions, she would cry.

"Hey, hey! I feel sorry for anyone who let you go from their lives. Honestly, I don't know how they get up in the morning..." I explained and continued, "You can't be scared of anyone or anything. And now not even from death."

"Huh?" She probably couldn't make sense of my last statement. So, I reached out for my backpack again, "This is also for you," I said, handing over a gift package to her.

"What is it?" She asked.

"Don't you want to see for yourself?" My feet became restless, and my stomach fell to my feet as she started unwrapping it. It was the second wave of emotional efflorescence that I had to endure that evening.

"Diary of a Whimsical Lover." She read out loud. "Oh! Your book! Congratulations." She hugged me.

"More like your book, Maya." She looked at my face as I spoke, silently asking me to elaborate. Her face was the most adorable and innocent thing I had seen in a long time.

"This is the first piece of literature ever written about you. There would be more coming. I told you there was so much to say..."

"What...what..." Her voice got muffled as she covered her mouth—something she did when she was startled. She kept looking at the front and back cover of the book and fluttering its pages in awe.

"And congratulations to you, for Maya has become immortal." I looked at her and smiled as her divine eyes met mine. And then she leaned towards my face. The bench we sat on suddenly hovered at first and then flew upwards, taking me to the clouds from where I could see an aerial view of the Central Park. And I saw seven or maybe twenty-seven rainbows on that bright sunny day. They weren't the usual ones with seven colors. I saw colors I didn't even know existed before. An eerie sound wave that grew louder with every passing second and before my ears began bleeding and my head exploded, I opened my eyes and found myself lying in my bed.

"Where is the bench? Where is she?" I murmured in confusion and instantly realized what had happened. It was almost five in the evening, and I had to meet Maya. I quickly put on my runners, grabbed the car keys, and picked up the book rushing downstairs without waiting for the elevator. As I descended the stairs, my mind wondered about the outcome. I couldn't get out of the car for several minutes after I parked it beside the running track, and the subdued thoughts grew louder in my head. Would it end the way it did in my dream, or would this evening change my life forever, flipping it upside down?

I finally stepped out of the car and started jogging on the trail with my book in my hand, hoping to catch Maya soon. After one complete lap of the park, I decided to look near the pond where she used to sit and watch ducks and geese playing in the water.

As soon as the excitement of finding her standing near the pond hit my nerves, I felt the ground beneath me slipping. Who is that guy? My brain tried to find the answer to my question. I recalled every cousin of hers, friends, anyone who I had seen in the past four years but couldn't figure out just who he was. Her eyes were fixed on his face, and she didn't blink for an entire minute.

I turned around, looking at the cover of my book and frowning upon my fate. Is that the end of it? Or an adventure called love has just begun? I wondered while sitting inside my car.

In a minute, everything was a blur—a distant unachievable dream. The thought of losing her had haunted me for long as a nightmarish vision of an inevitable force separating us—a passing thought that I could brush away. But here I was today, watching the horrors of a dystopian vision materialize itself into reality. I could feel my core temperature plummeting when a sudden thought crossed my mind. I knew I had to confess my love for her irrespective of the consequences. I had to give her the book, which was a testament to my love. Even if my dream did not come true, she would know that once upon a time, there was an admirer who got through his darkest hours with her as his only breath.

Her mere sight had given him hope in times the world came crashing down around him. She would know that in the crisis of human existence, she became the purpose he lived for. Even if she refused to reciprocate my love, her heart would never forget me as the person she saved by merely existing. As I mustered up all my courage and walked towards her, I felt the park gradually morph into a desolate cactus land, distorted chicanery forcing me to retreat. It was as if destiny was devising a plan to cause a hindrance, but I remained unperturbed. Love had taught me to break free of all my inhibitions, instilling the courage that I lacked.

She saw me walking straight to her from a distance and gently waved as I reached closer to hand her the book. She looked confused, and for the first time, my love for her made me courageous. My mind stopped reprimanding me for being an introvert for the first time. I felt relieved handing over my heart in her hands which had gotten too heavy to carry. At that moment, I realized I did not even care if she tossed it aside or accepted it because it was in her possession now anyway. At that moment, I made us infinite, and nobody could snatch that from me, not even her.

"Diary of a Whimsical Lover. What is this about?" She asked as she flicked through the pages frantically, till she turned to the first page, which read,

To my beloved, Maya–

Since I saw you from the window,
Across the block, beyond the cemetery.
Your innocence allured my being, instilled a mystery.
Tremors shook from my spine to the brain,
Little did I know; I will never be the same again.

This isn't an impression but expression,
Of feelings, love and a phase,
My attempt of retrogression,
Undoubtedly, without any expectation,
Hoping my dispossession, from the enchantment.

Dear Maya, this is a tale of a time blackened,
Something that never happened before, happened!

Acknowledgements

I would have taken much longer to complete this book if my sister, Mallika had not religiously encouraged me to work on it by asking, "When are you gonna finish that s#%t book?" So, thank you! Mallika.

And thanks for absolutely not forcing me to write this acknowledgement for you.

I would also like to thank literally no one else.

About the Author

Gaurav is a Delhi-born, Bihar-raised and Canada-based author. He studied journalism and business in college but practised neither. Gaurav used to follow some publishers but could never relate to them. So, he became one and founded Think Tank Books—he relates to him very well now.

When not writing or publishing books, he either overthinks about random stuff happening around him or passionately does the dishes.

He is on Instagram and Facebook (who isn't?) @authorgauravsharma. He also has a website, authorgauravsharma.com.

Also by the same author

Fiction (English)
1. *Long Live the Sullied (2020): The Sullied Warrior Duology Book 2*
2. *God of the Sullied (2018): The Sullied Warrior Duology Book 1*
3. *Gone are the Days (2016): Semi-autobiographical*

Fiction (Hindi)
1. *Charitranayak Eklavya (2020): Translation of God of the Sullied*
2. *Mahanayak Eklavya (2020): Translation of Long Live the Sullied*

Literary Criticism/Creative Non-fiction
1. *The Indian Story of an Author (2018): A blank book and symbolic protest*

Academic Textbooks
1. *Development and Communication Morphosis (2014)*
2. *Photography Redefined (2013)*
3. *Design and Graphics Redefined (2013)*

Edited Anthology
1. *None of a Kind (2020): A collection of 20 short stories written by 15 authors*

www.ingramcontent.com/pod-product-compliance
Lightning Source LLC
Chambersburg PA
CBHW020924160726
47993CB00005B/2119